PUFFIN BOOKS

AVALANCHE!

Avalanche! is an unusually fine story of quite desperate moments and deadly dangers bravely tackled. And it is mainly true. In any bad year, tons of snow may break loose and go thundering down from the high mountains on to little valleys where people are living. It was such a year when a party of boys and girls from the Pestalozzi Children's Village went to a high Alpine hut to ski. Their adventures began as avalanche after avalanche came down, slowly at first, then spreading and gaining speed till they hurtled down and down, over the hut and farther still. The position was desperate, but the children were brave, throwing in every scrap of endurance, strength, knowledge, and judgement. Being children they did not all have endurance and judgement, and none of them had them all the time, but they helped each other out, and came through triumphant.

The story is excellently translated from the Dutch, and was voted the Best Children's Book of the Year in Holland. The sheer excitement of scenes which seem completely true and natural carries the reader straight through from start to finish, but there are wonderful highlights of personality and scene which almost force you to go back and read the story again in case the first reading missed anything. It is a grand book, infectious in its feeling of courage in adventure, and is warmly recommended for boys and girls of eleven or twelve and upwards.

Cover design by Richard Kennedy

D0255831

A. Rutgers van der Loeff

AVALANCHE!

TRANSLATED FROM THE DUTCH BY
Dora Round

ILLUSTRATED BY
Alie Evers

PUFFIN BOOKS

Puffin Books, Penguin Books Ltd, Harmondsworth, Middlesex, England
Penguin Books, 625 Madison Avenue, New York, New York 10022, U.S.A.
Penguin Books Australia Ltd, Ringwood, Victoria, Australia
Penguin Books Canada Ltd, 2801 John Street, Markham, Ontario, Canada L3R 1B4
Penguin Books (N.Z.) Ltd, 182–190 Wairau Road, Auckland 10, New Zealand

—

First published in Holland 1954
This edition first published 1957
Published in Puffin Books 1959
Reprinted 1961, 1964, 1965, 1967, 1968, 1971 (twice), 1973, 1974,
1975, 1976, 1977, 1978, 1980, 1981

—

—

Made and printed in Great Britain
by Richard Clay (The Chaucer Press) Ltd,
Bungay, Suffolk
Set in Monotype Bembo

*In Holland in 1954 this book was awarded the title
The Best Children's Book of the Year*

CONTENTS

1	THE SNOW-BOUND VILLAGE	7
2	THE JOURNEY UP	16
3	THE BOYS FROM THE CHILDREN'S VILLAGE	24
4	THE WAY DOWN	30
5	THE NIGHT IT HAPPENED	39
6	UNDER THE SNOW	50
7	EVACUATION	61
8	PAOLO AND WERNER	72
9	THE TRAIN JOURNEY	89
10	NEWS ON THE WIRELESS	110
11	THE RESCUE	122
12	MARIE	142
13	WHERE DO WE GO FROM HERE?	151
14	THE CHILDREN'S VILLAGE	168

I

THE SNOW-BOUND VILLAGE

ON Monday January the seventeenth early in the morning it began to snow. It snowed and snowed, hour after hour, day and night. By Friday there were more than six feet of fresh snow on top of the old, hard-packed layer that had been lying there since December. And still it went on snowing.

But it seemed to be growing lighter. There was a change in the sky. By midday the snow had thinned to a few fluttering flakes, and for the first time for days one could see some distance.

The old people in the little mountain village of Urteli, now completely cut off by the snow, stared anxiously up at the steep slopes where the black patches of pine forest were now almost hidden under their thick white load, and the little haystacks and avalanche-breaks had completely disappeared. Screwing up their eyes in their wrinkled brown faces, they stared upwards. They shook their heads anxiously, looking more worried every hour. It was too mild for the time of year and the wind was changeable. Just like the year of disaster, 1927.

'Bad, very bad,' muttered John, the bent old road-mender. He had spent the whole day clearing a narrow path along what had been the village street, where the snow now lay in deep drifts between the houses.

'Hi! Look out!' shouted Bartel, the son of Gurtnelli the café owner. Bartel stood on the roof of the café up to his waist in snow, trying again, as he had every day, to shovel down some of the enormously heavy load of snow. But it was a hopeless task. The other villagers had given it up. At night they lay restlessly awake, thinking they heard the roof beams crack under the weight.

'I should call it a day if I were you!' Bartel shouted down to Old John. 'We'd better climb in through the first floor windows. It's much easier than grubbing passages to our front doors.'

But Old John only scowled and went on working away with his broad snow shovel.

'A man must work or else he starts thinking too much,' he grunted.

From time to time there came the heavy thump of the great lumps of snow as Bartel shovelled them off the roof of the café.

'The school kids are having a fine time! They haven't been to school for two days. I never had that when *I* was a kid!' shouted Bartel again. Up there on the roof his young voice would ordinarily have rung out clearly, but now with the thick heavy blanket of snow covering everything and dimming all sounds, his words came dully through the snowflakes that still fluttered slowly down.

'Children are children,' grunted Old John. 'They don't know what's in store for them.'

But Bartel did not hear him. 'I do believe the sun's going to come out,' he shouted. He pointed with outstretched arm to a pale, watery spot in the grey snow cloud.

'We must thank God if it stops snowing,' muttered Old John, looking up.

'Did you saying something?' called Bartel, shovelling down another huge block of snow.

But the old road-mender shook his head on its wry neck. 'You youngsters think you know everything,' he called up hoarsely. 'But the Kühelihorn and the Glarbeckscher will teach you something yet!'

'What?' laughed Bartel looking at the two eastern peaks. He could see them both from where he stood. 'They look quite good and quiet.'

'Oh, yes. Good and quiet. That's what you say,' grumbled Old John. He pulled out his large brown handkerchief to blow his nose. This he did at length and with great thoroughness. When he had finished he called: 'I'm going to find my old woman. She'll have the soup hot for my dinner by now, I expect.' And he trudged off with the broad snow shovel over his shoulder. Round a bend in the path he vanished between the high snow walls which reached to the wooden balconies of the upper storeys.

The villagers had managed to dig little passages running close round the houses from their front doors. A dim twilight showed through the panes of the ground floor windows, except where the heavy wooden shutters were closed and the attempt to clear the snow had been given up. In the little grocer's shop women with aprons over their black coats and shopping baskets on their arms stood gossiping in the feeble light of an unshaded electric bulb. Their faces under their woollen scarves were pale and serious.

'The baker's only got yeast enough to last for three days,' said one.

'Did you hear what the wireless said half an hour ago?' asked another.

Old John did not find his wife at home when he stepped into the dark kitchen. But the saucepan of soup stood on the oil stove. He took off the lid and sniffed.

'Lentil soup,' he murmured, 'but where are the onions?' He shook his head. Of course there were no onions left in the village. All supplies were cut off.

He found his old woman with her upstairs neighbour Mrs Rähmi, listening to the wireless. In this room too there was a strange, milky twilight. But on the table glowed the familiar green cloth with the red roses, and on it his wife's work-worn hands lay beside those of her younger neighbour. There was a restful look about those old hands, and in an odd way that comforted him.

He cleared his throat but his wife nodded silently at the wireless and signed to him to sit down. The clock struck twelve strokes. They took a long time. And after the last stroke it was a few seconds before the familiar voice of the announcer began:

'The Federal Research Institute into snow and avalanche conditions at Weissfluhjoch-Davos has issued the following statement. Since Monday night snow has been falling in the Alps without interruption, with westerly to northerly gales in places. In the Bernese Oberland, central Switzerland, and the Glarner Alps from five to eight feet of fresh snow have fallen during the last week. In the rest of the northern Alps, including Mittelbunden and Prätigau, from two and a half to five feet. There is acute danger of avalanches, especially in the central and eastern Alps. In many valleys they have already occurred, blocking roads and railways and carrying away the telephone wires. In some places the electricity supply is threatened. In view of the continued snowfall and the unfavourable winds and temperatures, people living in the area between the eastern frontier and the Bernese Oberland are strongly advised to take all necessary measures to evacuate houses and villages in places of danger. The threat of avalanches increases hourly. In the event of incidents, dial number eleven for information as to the nearest post where dogs are stationed.'

Mrs Rähmi turned off the wireless. She was pale and her lips quivered. 'I can't listen any more,' she said. 'I'm afraid. For the children.'

Old John glanced at the cradle in the corner by the stove and then at the toddler sitting under the table beside his mother's black-stockinged legs, spooning dried peas from one handleless cup into another and back again.

'It won't come to that,' he said, and added, 'I'm hungry.'

His wife got up without a word and the two old people shuffled through the door. Old John stuck his head in again to say with a shy, crooked smile: 'There's no harm packing your box in case we have to leave the village. You may as well be prepared. And a trip down the valley isn't bad for a change.'

Mrs Rähmi looked at him and said nothing. Then she got up with a jerk. Her foot knocked against the cup which the little boy had just painstakingly filled with dried peas, and he set up a yell like a pig being killed. His mother hauled him up by the seat of his pants and Old John laughed and shook his head.

'Not three yet and such a voice? If you hold him out of the window he'll start off an avalanche with his bellowing.' Then he vanished in search of his lentil soup.

But what he said was true.

Even a shout can do it. The silliest trifle can suddenly loosen the treacherously piled mass of snow and start it roaring down the slope in a cloud of dust, sweeping away everything in its path and crashing down to the valley, bringing white death where it comes. When the wind builds strange snow terraces up in the mountain tops and piles layer upon layer of snow of varying densities so that they can only just hold together, it creates a dangerous state of tension in which the slightest disturbance can make the whole thing break loose; the weight of a man or a chamois, even a vibration in the air, the sound of the wind, or a shout, is enough to tear the sloping masses apart and send them hissing and clattering down to the depths.

All the older people in the village knew this. So next day Hans Altschwank, who was schoolmaster and bell-ringer, decided not to ring in the Sunday rest as he usually did when work ended on a Saturday. He was afraid the sound of the bell would start the loose snow slipping on the steep slopes.

'It's the first time I haven't rung in the Sunday rest in all the years I've lived here,' he said sadly to Old John when he met him in the narrow path along the village street. 'The first time in nearly twenty years.'

Ever since Hans Altschwank had been schoolmaster he had rung the bell of the humble little grey stone church at Urteli.

The village had no minister and no sexton. It was too poor and too small. But the minister came up from Glarmatt twice a week, one of these visits being on Sunday afternoon to preach a sermon. This week, of course, it was impossible for him to come up.

'Have you heard?' called Finetti, the butcher and sausage-maker, hobbling along quickly to meet them in his blood-stained apron and pulling down the sleeves of his thick grey jersey with impatient tugs as he came. 'They're beginning to evacuate the women and children from here early on Monday. They've all got to go. First to Glarmatt and then further down the valley by train. The troops are coming up to help get them away. And the sappers are going to throw up breastworks and then let off mines and bring the dangerous avalanches down off the Kühelihorn and the Glarbeckscher that way. Tomorrow some time in the afternoon they'll be here. Perhaps my boy will be with them. He's down in Glarmatt doing his refresher course.'

'And you're glad?' asked Old John angrily. 'Man, go back to your sausage making. The lads will want a good feed.'

Finetti blew out his cheeks and cast up his eyes, a habit to which the villagers were accustomed. No one took any notice of it any more.

Hans Altschwank shrugged his shoulders and said: 'We must take things as they are. Let Finetti look forward to seeing his son if he wants to.'

A boy of about fifteen came running after them. He had a brown face with rosy cheeks under the woollen cap with ear-flaps which he wore like everyone else in the village. He seemed excited. He screwed up his eyes against the first pale rays of the sun which were struggling through the grey blanket of cloud now that the snow had stopped.

'Dad!' he called from a few yards away. Hans Altschwank turned.

'What's up, Werner?'

'The wireless says we must evacuate the village. Mr Baumgartner's going from house to house to see that everyone knows. Only people with cattle to tend may stay behind. May I stay, Dad?'

'I thought you wanted to see the world, boy. It isn't every day you get a chance to go down to the valley.'

'I'd rather stay up here,' said Werner shortly.

'You can't always choose,' said his father with equal shortness. 'Come along, we're going home.'

'There's something else, Dad,' said the boy as they turned for home.

Finetti and Old John looked after them. The schoolmaster and his son were about the same height, but the father was broader and his neck was brown and weatherbeaten. Both had the same quiet walk and the same sturdy legs. They walked close together between the high snow walls.

'There go the two best ski-runners in the village,' said Old John, looking after them.

'Yes, now my son isn't here,' said Finetti.

'Oh, get back to your sausage making,' said the old man. He rubbed his crooked nose with his finger, looked up at the Kühelihorn and the Glarbeckscher, shook his head again and grumbled: 'We ought to be off by now.'

Finetti blew out his cheeks. Then he turned and hobbled back to his shop. The woman waiting there might like another bit of news to gossip about. Old John plodded along thoughtfully, his shovel over his shoulder.

*

At home Hans Altschwank and his son sat at the table and silently ate up their soup. Altschwank thoughtfully crumbled a piece of bread; his face was grave. When the bread was all in crumbs his wife got up angrily.

'Why don't either of you say anything? You get on my nerves and no wonder!' She swept all the breadcrumbs off the table into her hand and threw them irritably into her husband's soup. 'Soon we shall have no bread at all,' she said. Then she covered her face with her hands and burst into sobs. 'I know you two are planning something you won't tell me about. As if everything wasn't difficult enough without that!'

Werner stirred his soup; he felt awkward and did not dare look up. His father went on with his meal in silence. When he had finished he pushed his plate to one side and put his arms on the table and looked straight at his wife.

'You're right, Mother. Werner and I are planning something. You know that hut half-way up to the Tschauschegg? Well, those boys must be still up there. No one's seen them since Monday. They'll have stayed inside all through this heavy snowfall, of course. But it's lasted so long. They'll be running short of food and they don't know what's been happening. They've no wireless there. Today or tomorrow they're bound to come down, because they must, and they'll come back to the village the usual way. Their leader knows, of course, that all this fresh snow isn't very healthy to go through, but he can't know how dangerous things are at the moment. And he can't know this village is to be evacuated. Werner and I are going up there this afternoon; we shall go the long way round by the Breitlibach and then over the ridge. You needn't be anxious – there's no danger of avalanches there. We must show them that way down, because if they try to come the other way and cross that great flat stretch of snow below the Kühelihorn they'll be buried by an avalanche before they know where they are.'

'But why must you two be the ones to go?'

'Why not?' he asked gently.

'Let them go hungry for a day or two!' she begged.

'I would, if that was all,' said her husband. 'But we can't risk letting them start coming down on their own, or something frightful may happen, and it won't happen only to them. Our village is being evacuated because it's in danger. Whatever happens we must see that an avalanche isn't started off just a day too soon.'

'You needn't be frightened, Mother,' said Werner. 'Dad and I will be careful.'

'Oh, child, what do you know about the mountains!'

Werner reddened but said nothing.

'We'll take care of ourselves,' said his father. 'We'll use avalanche cords and each carry a spade. Nothing'll happen to us.' He spoke in a tone which told his wife that further argument was useless. She dried her eyes on her apron, pressed her lips tightly together and set about stacking the plates.

'Come along, Werner, we'll get ready,' said Altschwank. 'Mother, if we're not home before dark you'll know we're spending the night at the hut and that you must feed the animals. Mind you close and bar the shutters tight. And if you can manage it, drop in and see Aunt Augusta. She's as pig-headed as they're made: she'll never agree to be evacuated.'

'She'll have to,' said his wife bitterly, 'like all the rest of us.'

2

THE JOURNEY UP

THEY had no proper avalanche cord. This is strong red rope marked off at every five yards, but the villagers did not use it. 'Newfangled stuff, all right for crazy skiers and tourists,' said the people of Urteli. 'Let them run around trailing a tail like that behind them if they want to. We can manage without. Like our grandfathers . . .'

'We'll get some stuff we can use from Aunt Augusta's shop,' Hans Altschwank said to his son. They slipped along the narrow path one behind the other on their skis.

Aunt Augusta kept the village drapery store, a dark little shop where she sold bootlaces and press-studs, shirts, pants and aprons, tape, apron-strings and yarn. All by touch. She seemed able to smell out anything she wanted. Her customers could hardly make out what was stacked in the dark corners and dangled from the rafters above the tiny counter. They were accustomed to waiting patiently in the half-darkness which smelled of starch and new, unwashed clothes. Now and then she would move a whole lot of cardboard boxes to another place for no apparent reason, or climb with her old bandy legs up a rickety ladder that had been creaking and wobbly for years, but she seemed to like that. It was the music that suited her. She refused to accept the new ladder which had been standing ready for her in Altschwank's barn for a long time now.

Werner and his father stuck their skis upright in the snow beside the shop door. The snow wall on either side reached almost to the low roof, where the snow was piled so thickly that it looked like a gigantic feather bed, freshly plumped up, and reached almost to the thick layer of snow on the neighbouring houses, completely darkening the small space between. In front of the door they scraped the snow off their boots and brushed them with the straw besom that stood ready. Then one behind the other they stepped inside.

'Have you wiped your feet?' asked Aunt Augusta in her creaky voice. Winter and summer she asked everyone who came into the shop if he had wiped his feet. The villagers had stopped answering the question long ago.

'We want two hundred yards of strong braid or binding from you, Auntie,' said her nephew. 'You'd better begin with all the red and after that all the other bright colours you've got.'

'What did you say?' asked his aunt.

Altschwank patiently repeated what he wanted. Aunt Augusta wasn't deaf, far from it, but life's surprises were sometimes too much for her. To explain things he added: 'We're going to fetch a party of boys from the hut before it's too late. We want to use your stuff as avalanche ropes.'

'As what?'

'Avalanche ropes. To be on the safe side. It ought to be strong red cord marked in lengths. You tie it round your waist and let about twenty yards trail behind you. If anything happens and you're buried under the snow, your friends find the end of the rope. They can tell from the markings on it where to look for you.'

'Nonsense,' said Aunt Augusta. 'Newfangled nonsense. My grandfather was flung from the roof of his house by an avalanche and buried six hundred yards lower down. He dug himself out without so much as a cold in the head. But nowadays! All this fancy nonsense they have to have or they fall down and stub their toes. Must I give my braid that cost good money for that?'

'This modern nonsense has saved a good many lives,' said her nephew. 'Come along and give us all the bright coloured stuff you've got.'

Aunt Augusta grunted and began to climb her creaking ladder, grumbling as she went. Presently she dumped some cards of strong, brightly coloured cotton apron strings and a couple of rolls of broad red and green braid in front of him.

'Try and keep it clean,' she snapped. 'Then you can bring it back. I can easily run an iron over it.'

Hans Altschwank smiled. He knew she wasn't really a bad old soul. But he did not answer. He stuffed everything into his knapsack in silence. He and Werner had each a short shovel and two loaves in their knapsacks besides. It had been hard work getting the baker to part with the bread.

'Soon we shan't have enough for our own people,' he objected.

'What d'you mean, our own people?' Werner heard his father ask. 'Aren't the boys up there people, too?'

'Did you see them? Did you hear them?' demanded the baker indignantly. 'They're foreign brats! I've never heard so much queer babble in all my life. Sometimes they can't even understand each other! Then they all start speaking German. And some of them speak Italian too.'

'So what?' asked Altschwank.

'Nothing,' said the baker. 'In normal times I bake bread for everyone, all customers are the same to me. But in times of shortage I bake for my own people first. I just want you to know.'

Hans Altschwank shrugged his shoulders. Werner picked up the loaves which the baker handed over with an ill grace, and stuffed them into the knapsacks.

'We've got quite a job before us,' said Altschwank as they fastened on their skis again outside Aunt Augusta's door. 'We shall have to do the climb without skins. If anything happens, we can get away much quicker with no skins on our skis. We shall have to keep our distance, too, as soon as we start climbing. Fifty yards between us. And if I stop, you stop. If I swing my arm twice, unfasten your skis. If I swing it three times you can fasten them again. We're taking a safe route but we must be careful of snow shelves breaking away. And mind: off with your skis and fling away your sticks as soon as you see you can't get through. If the snow comes over you, swim as hard as you can. Tread with your feet and swim with your arms – it helps to keep you up.'

'Oh, I know all that, Dad.' Werner was impatient.

'You can't hear it too often. It hasn't happened to you yet. It needs a lot of practice before you do the right thing automatically. Plenty of experienced mountaineers have been killed because they didn't fling off their skis at once. Skis and sticks anchor you fast under the snow. And remember: if you're buried by the snow, keep your hand in front of your nose and mouth and shove your elbows out in front to make a breathing space. And don't panic. Keep calm. If we keep our distance we can't both be buried at once.'

Werner glided silently behind his father. He was glad no one saw them go, or they would have had the whole village giving them advice. Dad had chosen his time well, just after dinner.

In a few minutes they reached the last houses and the end of the path through the village. They climbed sideways up the high snow wall. Then their tracks cut deep into the loose white snow, which had just frozen over on the surface and broke through with a soft crack under their skis. It was hard work for the leader. Slowly they climbed higher. The familiar slopes lay before them looking strange and quite deserted. Most of the landmarks were covered by the snow. Here and there the wind had blown two overhanging layers together, making queer, unfamiliar shapes with blue shadows. The Kühelihorn and the Glarbeckscher looked down upon them threateningly. There was something awe-inspiring about it all. Werner felt strangely excited.

He was glad he had spoken to his father about the boys in the hut. No one else in the village had remembered them.

Werner had only seen them once, on the Saturday before the snow began. They were very ordinary boys, probably on a ski-ing trip with a teacher, perhaps from some boarding school. They had come through the village on their way up from Glarmatt to the hut. They had bought bread at the baker's, and oranges and chocolate at Klugi's. That was where he had seen them. They were all talking German. After that he had seen them climbing the slopes above in a long line, one behind the other, all with heavy knapsacks. He had not counted them but there were certainly ten of them. He had gone to chop wood for his mother, and later when he glanced up from the back yard he saw them like a row of black dots high up on the hillside. The sun was still shining that day and it looked as if the weather would be lovely. But those boys had not had much fun out of their ski-ing holiday.

Suddenly his father called back to him:

'We'll rope up with the avalanche cords now.'

They chose the strong red apron strings that Aunt Augusta had given them. Each of them let an end twenty yards long trail behind him. It made Werner feel more excited still. They didn't talk much. Below them to one side lay the village, sunk deep in the snow, unrecognizable. On the roofs lay the thick, shining white cushions with dark shadows between, and from the chimneys rose thin columns of dirty grey smoke.

Werner looked up. He could see the hut lying like a black speck in all that whiteness. It seemed silly to have to go such a long way round to get there. Ordinarily it would mean an hour's climb. But now? Along the Breitlibach and over the ridge – without skins on their skis.

'It doesn't look dangerous, Dad,' he said. There was a catch in his voice though he tried to make it sound light.

'We'll keep our distance now, fifty yards,' was the abrupt answer. 'And mind, all that I was telling you was just in case. You needn't be afraid.'

'I'm not afraid!' said Werner indignantly.

They were climbing more steeply now. Werner kept fifty yards behind. He looked behind him once. The village had grown much smaller. From up here you could hardly see it. Just some white humps in two neat rows on either side of the village street. When you were down there it looked much untidier. He shook his head, feeling a little sorry for his village. It looked so small.

'I don't believe anything's going to happen,' he murmured as if to reassure himself. Then he looked up at the white peaks. 'Nothing at all,' he muttered, wrinkling up his forehead.

He remembered the date carved on his home: 1672. It had stood there all those hundreds of years. And there were other houses as old as that in the village. Nineteen twenty-seven had been a year of frightful disaster, he knew that, but no one had been killed and hardly any cattle, and the damaged houses and stables had all been rebuilt, better and more modern ones than before. Then why were people so frightened?

Suddenly there was a soft rumbling noise. Werner saw his father stop. The sound came from the further side of the valley. Hans Altschwank pointed with his stick. Down the steep side of the Hörnigen slid an avalanche. Before you could count three, the shining white wall was marked with a widening streak of dirty grey. The soft rumble grew to a swelling roar. Werner turned cold. Luckily there were no houses or cow-sheds there, perhaps it was a well-known avalanche slide. Though he could not see well from where he stood, he knew that it must have brought down a lot of trees, rocks and rubble with it.

He glanced at his father, who swung his stick again as a sign that they should go on. At that moment Werner hated the fifty yards that separated them. He was not really afraid, but that short and terrible roar in the deathly stillness of the valley had made him feel cold.

The journey seemed to go on for hours. Again and again his father stopped. He chose his way with the greatest care.

Climbing without skins was hard work. Again and again their skis tried to slip backwards. They had to climb whole stretches by setting their skis herringbone-wise in the snow. Hans Altschwank set a good pace. After a bit Werner felt the sweat pouring down his face. His shirt stuck to his back. The physical effort was so great that he forgot his fear and hardly remembered to keep his distance. He was surprised when they suddenly stood on the ridge. He drew a deep breath. The hut now lay at about the same height and on their left. They would have to walk some distance up the gentle slope of the ridge and then glide smoothly down to the hut.

His father signed to him to stay there while he himself went on. Werner saw him moving his skis very carefully. Was he trying to start an avalanche now so as to make the return journey safer? An avalanche now, starting from here, would do no damage on its way down. But nothing happened. Werner was not surprised. The Tschauschegger was reckoned a safe mountain with ideal ski-ing slopes – at least under normal conditions.

Altschwank signed to his son to come on. Werner moved forward with some difficulty. It was only now that he felt how tired he was from this forced climb and how his arms ached from using his stick too much. But he laughed. They were nearly there.

In front of the hut he saw tiny black figures shovelling away the snow. They must have worked hard to keep the snow from piling up all round the hut. If they had not done that they would have had to sit in the dark all day. They would not have enough oil to keep their lamp alight through the day.

His father started off on the run down. He shot slantwise across the slope, ending just in front of the door of the hut, where he stopped abruptly with a short turn. Werner grinned. It was a pity he couldn't hear what the boys said in their astonishment.

A few minutes later he came whizzing down, stopped with

a model *Christiana*, and looked round with a triumphant grin at the brown faces of a group of boys younger than himself. And then he felt he must have been set down on the Tower of Babel. He had hardly said 'Hullo!' when they all started shouting in every language on earth. A very dark boy slapped him on the back, stumbling over his words so that it was some time before he said anything intelligible.

'My name's Nikolai Kastopoulos,' he said in good German. 'I'm Greek and we come from the Pestalozzi village at Trogen.'

The Pestalozzi village! He might have thought of that before, when the baker spoke of foreign brats. Foreign brats indeed! Tomorrow he, Werner Altschwank, would tell the baker what he thought of him. Dad shouldn't have let him get away with that sort of talk.

He stood his skis against the wall of the hut among the others and let himself be drawn by the crowd of pushing, excited boys, shouting in half a dozen languages at once, into the hut where his father was talking to the leader of the expedition, a very tall middle-aged man with a friendly face.

3

THE BOYS FROM THE CHILDREN'S VILLAGE

They drank hot tea made of lime blossom but without lemon, for the lemons were finished long ago. The bread was received with shouts of joy, cut into thick hunks and polished off at once.

'All we've got left is a bag of oatmeal and a yard of mountain sausage,' a tall, dark boy confided to Werner. He was the quietest of them and seemed to be a Finn. His name was Antti Rananjärvi. Werner found this rather a mouthful to remember all at once, but he liked the boy. Really, he liked them all.

They overwhelmed him with questions about the weather reports and what they said about the snow. He told them what he knew. The wireless had been broadcasting a weather bulletin every hour for the last few days. The news that this particular valley was especially dangerous because the abnormally heavy snowfall had concentrated on this part of the Alps, seemed to delight the boys instead of alarming them. Only Antti, the tall Finn, looked serious.

'Don't take any notice of him,' cried a little Italian, 'he's always serious.'

Antti grinned briefly and shook his head.

'What were you all planning to do?' Werner asked. 'You must have been jolly hungry.'

'Hungry!' said one of them. 'We've all been much hungrier than this.' He was called Jean Pierre and came from Marseilles. He was short and rather broad, and probably looked older than he really was. His lips curled a little scornfully at the word 'hungry' and he pointed to a length of sausage that still hung from a nail.

'Mr Hutamäki is no fool,' said another boy. 'He put us on half rations. And as we couldn't go on any ski-ing trips we didn't get so very hungry.'

'H'm,' said Werner.

He looked at the man talking to his father. So that was Mr Hutamäki, another outlandish name. Perhaps he was a Finn too. Hans Altschwank and Mr Hutamäki sat in a corner in earnest conversation with their backs half turned to the boys. When two boys went up to them to ask something they were waved away in a decided manner.

'Mr Hutamäki is in charge of our house,' said Antti with a glance at him. 'That's the Finnish house. We each have our own house in our village. The Italians and Greeks have two houses each. And we all have a foster father and mother in charge of the house who are our teachers as well. We're war orphans, you see.' He said this shyly, as if being an orphan were something to be ashamed of.

Werner nodded. 'I know about that,' he said. 'We planted fruit trees for you here in our valley and in summer we sell the fruit and the money goes to the Pestalozzi village. Just like the other Swiss children. But I'm afraid we don't help you very much. Between you and me, the apples are simply foul. It's too high here to get good fruit and the ground is poor. But Dad wanted us to do like all the others. Dad is the school-master, you see.'

When boys say 'you see' to each other it's because they are shy, and they are always shy of talking about themselves. So they moved away from these personal details as quickly as they could and talked about the sausage. All the boys were talking about the sausage. Now that they were leaving, the sausage must be finished up. The thin length hanging from the nail drew their attention like a magnet.

'Hans Peter, ask if we may share out the sausage.'

Hans Peter was an Austrian. He was the eldest of the boys and had come with them to help Mr Hutamäki. In the village

he was not one of the children but an assistant in the clothing store, where he made shelves and cupboards and helped with the sorting.

'Just wait quietly,' he said calmly.

The little Italian, whose liveliness had caught Werner's attention at once, was jumping up and down like an excited monkey and letting loose a flood of Italian which he broke off to shout in German and French: 'Oh, do let's go now, do let's go now!'

'We've been shut up here for five days, we can wait another hour,' answered Hans Peter comfortably.

'Boys!' said Mr Hutamäki, unfolding himself to his full length and running a hand over his shock of grey hair. 'We're leaving here as soon as all knapsacks are properly packed and the hut tidied up. Let's say in a quarter of an hour. Keep calm and do as I've taught you!' he added in a sudden bellow as the boys began to shout and jump about excitedly.

The hut looked remarkably tidy, seeing that eleven people had lived in it for a week. Hans Peter said what each one was to do.

'Antti put out the fire. Jean Pierre and François sweep out the hut. Martin and Holdert wash out those bowls. Paolo keep out of everyone's way if you can.'

The last words were greeted with a roar of laughter and Paolo flung his arms before his face and pretended to burst into loud sobs. The others set about packing and seeing that the bunks were left tidy.

'And mind you don't hide any dirt and rubbish in corners or sweep it under the benches!' ordered Hans Peter.

He winked at Werner. They were about the same age and felt years wiser than these excited twelve-, thirteen- and fourteen-year-olds. Only Antti was as much as fifteen.

'The older boys couldn't get away,' Antti explained to Werner. 'They get technical training at Trogen, some of them are apprenticed. But I'm at the high school at St Gall.'

'Well, they won't envy you now,' said Werner. 'Your ski-ing holiday is spoilt.'

'They'll be very anxious about us,' answered Antti with a worried look. 'We haven't been able to write all this time, and the wireless reports haven't been exactly reassuring. I expect Mr Hutamäki will send a telegram as soon as we get down.'

Werner shook his head. 'He won't be able to,' he said. 'The wires are down. The wireless say the Post Office engineers are working like blazes to repair as much as possible, but a tiny place like our village will have to wait its turn. The soldiers are coming tomorrow. They'll have their own transmitter. Perhaps they can get a message through for you.'

Twenty minutes of noise and excitement and running to and fro seemed really to achieve a result; the knapsacks were packed and everything was reasonably tidy. Mr Hutamäki hammered on the table with his fist to get everyone's attention.

'Now you all just keep your mouths shut and listen as you have never listened in your lives before to what Mr Altsch-wank here has to say to you. He's going to lead us down by a route we don't know but where we shall have the least chance of unpleasant surprises. If you follow his instructions exactly – and mind, I mean *exactly* – nothing can happen to us. But remember, our lives may depend on it.' Mr Hutamäki, whose face was so wrinkled that it looked rather strange at first glance, looked at his party so anxiously that one or two of the boys started to giggle nervously. Others gazed gravely back at him. They all felt the tension.

'Go ahead,' said Hutamäki to Hans Altschwank.

Altschwank repeated everything that he had said to his son a couple of hours earlier. He impressed upon the boys all the precautions they must take whenever they ran the least risk of coming on to ground where an avalanche might be started. He dealt out a length of coloured apron string to each of them to tie on and pay out as soon as they were spaced out at fifty yards. This caused some suppressed exclamations of delight, though here and there a face turned pale. Werner noticed that the noisy little Italian boy's chin was quivering as he fastened his on his knapsack. He decided to stay near the child. That meant that he would be the one to follow Paolo fifty yards behind.

'I say, how old are you?' he asked Paolo when they were putting on their skis outside the hut.

'What's that got to do with you?' asked Paolo loftily.

'Oh well, it's a thing one asks about puppies,' answered Werner a little crossly. He was attracted by the boy, though he did not know why.

'I'm not a puppy, I'm a boy,' said Paolo with dignity.

'There's nothing to be afraid of,' said Werner kindly, noticing the look of strain on the little brown face.

'I've been buried once already,' said Paolo suddenly in a high, quivering voice. 'Under the rubble. When our cellar was blown in during the war. I don't want to be buried again.' His lips were quivering as well now.

Werner felt helpless. 'Look here, Paolo,' he said, 'my Dad and I have just climbed up here to fetch you down safely. Don't panic. Roping up with avalanche cord doesn't mean a thing – at sea you have to do boat drill however fine the weather is. You do it to please my Dad.'

One by one they started. The fifty yards were roughly judged. Mr Hutamäki was to come last. Werner took care to go immediately after Paolo. The little Italian boy took off quickly. He could ski quite well, that was clear. Mr Hutamäki must have brought only the best skiers. In easy curves they followed the trail of Hans Altschwank's skis. The powdery snow spurted up in clouds. Anyone who did not know would have thought it an ideal ski-ing trip.

4

THE WAY DOWN

THE distance that had taken Werner and his father two hours to climb was covered in less than ten minutes. Everything went all right till suddenly there was a soft and menacing *woooom!* For a breadth of seventy yards the snow broke away and a whole layer pitched downwards in a cloud of dust. Altschwank shouted something up to them but no one could understand him. Werner and Paolo found themselves in the path of the avalanche but fairly well to the side. Werner turned like lightning and shot away out of the danger zone. He had no time to shout to Paolo and it would have been no use. At the critical moment the child looked round helplessly, saw the foaming white mass bearing down on him, heard the swish and roar. He could have shot away to the other side out of danger more easily even than Werner, but in his terror he made a wrong movement and fell. This was the worst thing that could have happened. He could not get rid of his skis and sticks now. His shriek sounded faintly, dulled by the billowing snow.

The whole thing happened in a twinkling. It was only a small avalanche on a slope that was not very steep. Everyone who was not paralysed with terror hurried to the spot near to which Paolo must lie buried. Mr Hutamäki was there first and Antti second. Werner struggled frantically up the slope, eager to lend a hand at once with the shovel that he carried in his knapsack. By the time Hans Altschwank got back to them, his anxious face dripping with sweat, they had found the end of the red apron string that Paolo was using as an avalanche cord. It was not marked, so they did not know in which direction to search. Altschwank pointed with his stick. That was probably the place. To be on the safe side they hunted feverishly in both directions.

'Careful!' shouted Altschwank. 'Mind that thing doesn't break! It's not real avalanche cord and the snow's heavy.'

After about five minutes they found the place where Paolo must be lying. Nearly twenty yards of the red string were cleared of snow. Five of them worked together, Werner and his father, Mr Hutamäki, Antti and an Italian boy called Giuseppe. Altschwank and Mr Hutamäki ordered the others to keep their distance.

Side by side in a row they took soundings, using their sticks reversed and driving them deep in the snow, taking care to keep them vertical.

Suddenly Werner saw something. A small, dark point.

'There! There!' he shouted. 'I can see the point of his ski!'

A little later they found him. Antti was the first to feel him with his stick. He wasn't deep. They began to dig him out.

It was all a matter of seconds. It happened in a flash.

Woooommm! sounded for the second time.

'Clear out, all of you!' shouted Altschwank.

Some more snow broke away and came sliding down in a crumbling mass of whiteness, sending up clouds of dusty snow. Werner could have got away like the others, but he caught sight of a small brown hand that moved in the snow. He gripped the fingers with his left hand, ducked his face into his elbow, and held up his right arm with the shovel. 'I'm crazy,' he thought. 'This is the stupidest thing I could possibly do.'

He knew it was only a little avalanche. All the same he felt the snow lying on him like a heavy weight and pressing in on him from all sides like a cramping strait jacket. He lay in a wretched position, only breathing was easy. He felt that his left leg was twisted, but strangely enough he had no pain. Without realizing it, he still clung fast to Paolo's fingers.

He had no idea how long it lasted. He thought of all sorts of things – only not about Paolo, who was the reason why he had done it. He saw his father's perspiring face close to him and he saw the soup plate he had stared at while his father told his mother that they were going to fetch the boys from the hut. And he saw his mother's hands and her apron as she buried her face in it. He saw Aunt Augusta; she was busy ironing out the apron strings that she had lent them, so that she could still sell them. And he saw the calf that had broken a leg while it was being driven down the village street the week before and had had to be killed by Finetti.

It was easy to breathe and yet he felt himself growing hazy. It was dreadful not be to able to move. He didn't think about Paolo at all. Silly, he thought, it isn't white or black in front of my eyes but red. Red. He kept on thinking about that red colour. It was all very queer.

He began to get drowsy. But I'm not dying, he thought. We can't possibly be very deep under the snow. They must get us soon. Though he hardly remembered Paolo, he thought 'us' and not 'me'. We *can't* be very deep, he thought again. Silly not to be able to shout. Silly that the snow is so heavy.

Suddenly he felt a push. A minute later he saw light. He heard sounds. His head was dug out first.

'We've got him!' someone yelled. It was Giuseppe. Werner saw a shining wet face close to his own, black and brown against the white. He tried to smile but he couldn't. His face hurt. Some of the skin had come off.

He caught sight of his father. 'It's all right, Dad,' he whispered.

'You're as pig-headed as a . . . as pig-headed . . .' But his father could not finish. His voice was harsh and it trembled.

It turned out afterwards that Werner had only been buried for about seven minutes. Quite soon they had come upon the shovel pushed up through the snow.

'You can thank Heaven you're alive,' Werner's father told

him, 'because you did everything wrong. Except with the shovel.'

When Werner turned, Paolo was lying beside him in the snow. He did not move. Someone took off their skis for them. By the time Werner had dragged himself up with difficulty, sinking deep into the snow and gritting his teeth so as not to cry out with the pain in his thigh, the others were busy dealing with Paolo. Mr Hutamäki and Altschwank worked on him with artificial respiration. Then Hans Peter came up with a little mirror and held it in front of Paolo's mouth. The surface clouded over.

'That doesn't tell us much,' grumbled Altschwank. 'Let's hope he hasn't got snow in his lungs.'

But the position in which they found Paolo was not too bad. He seemed to have remembered at the last minute what he ought to do. He had managed to fling away his sticks and had held his arms in front of his face.

In less than ten minutes he began to breathe normally again and looked at his rescuers with a rather glassy eye. Unlike Werner, whose forehead and chin were badly skinned, he seemed to have suffered little damage. But instead of being brown his face was grey. Giuseppe and Hans Peter, Mr Hutamäki and Altschwank worked away at him, panting with their exertions. They rubbed his legs and arms, massaged his muscles and carefully tried all his joints.

At last he began to smile. But the smile changed to a quivering of his whole face and the quivering gave place to weeping. First he cried gently, but gradually his sobs grew fiercer and more miserable. Giuseppe stood up and said in a tone of mingled scorn and relief:

'This little flea will cry himself into jumping form all right.'

'Can you stand up, d'you think?' asked Mr Hutamäki shortly from his great height.

Paolo nodded, still sobbing. He scrambled up. Hans Peter helped him in silence. Paolo sank to his knees in the snow and fell over again. He looked round helplessly at the others and began to laugh. His face was an odd mixture of happiness and misery. Even Werner could not help smiling in spite of his painful face. But he stood there, silent and stiff, though he felt himself trembling inside.

Suddenly he found his father looking at him. He pulled himself together.

'Feel all right? Got pain anywhere?' His father's voice sounded worried.

'No,' said Werner. 'Only my leg. I've strained a muscle or something.'

'Can you do the last bit alone? We're nearly there.'

The village was in fact a few hundred yards away. Just a gentle slope to go down and they would be there.

'Can you stand on your skis?' Altschwank asked Paolo.

'*Sí, sí!*' Paolo assured him eagerly. The others heaved him up, planted him on his skis and fastened them. Werner took his knapsack. The straps were too short and cut him under the arms.

They pushed off quietly. Altschwank stayed beside Paolo and held him by the arm. He looked back once: at the tracks they had made on the way down, at the hut which showed like a black speck on the Tschauschegg, at the churned-up snow of the avalanche, which looked so small and innocent in the white expanse of the gentle slope but bore witness, with its roughly dug holes, to a terror which none of them would ever forget.

The rest of the party were waiting for them at the entrance to the village. They had taken off their avalanche cords and Antti stood holding the bunch of damp apron strings like a withered bouquet. They looked depressed. Only Giuseppe was speaking with suppressed vehemence to the group of shocked and silent boys.

It wasn't only the accident which had made them so low-spirited, it was the sight of the village which they had seen looking so different a week before. The houses were buried in snow for more than half their height, the roofs were piled incredibly high with snow which projected beyond them on all sides, casting strange deep shadows in the late light. The lower cowsheds and barns behind the houses seemed lost altogether under the lumpy white blanket. The snow was piled high on window sills and balconies, so that the fronts of the houses all looked out of drawing.

It was deathly still. Only a little boy with a black dog was climbing on all fours over a hillock of snow, sinking in deeply at each step. The dog barked, a high, yapping sound. There was nothing else to be heard. The villagers stayed within doors, living in fear.

Werner, to whom all this was familiar, glided past the others, glad to be there at last. At the mouth of the narrow path through the village he took off his skis and put them over his shoulder, But walking came harder than ski-ing. He felt as if he were hobbling. The others followed him, moving through the village street in the twilight like a row of snails. They saw lights in the houses and people moving, but there was no sound.

Suddenly a window was flung open and the smell of burnt porridge streamed out. It was like coming out of a bad dream. A woman stood at the window and called something. The boys began to talk softly among themselves. Paolo's shrill voice rang out suddenly. He said something in Italian and Giuseppe burst out laughing. Some of the others who had understood began to grin. Werner made a face. A plucky kid, Paolo, but in everyday life he must be a handful. All the same, he couldn't help liking him.

'Werner!' came his father's deep voice. 'We're going to ask if they can spend the night in Taureggi's cowshed. There's plenty of room there, more than in ours.'

Werner stopped and looked round. He looked straight into two black eyes belonging to Paolo, who was walking just in front of Altschwank. Paolo half tumbled, but it looked as if he had done it for fun, not in earnest. His curly black hair was in a tangle and his arms dangled limply. His eyes looked like a feverish child's, but there was a gleam in them which looked much more like a healthy young street arab. Werner looked away from those eyes which held a whole strange world. They embarrassed him. He felt a fool beside this lively boy with his tricks, he could not make him out, but he liked him.

'If you want to go straight home, do,' he heard his father say.

But he shook his head. He wanted to know if Taureggi could put the boys up for the night.

Altschwank went into a large dark house, the largest in the village. Heavy green shutters were closed across the windows. The walls were covered with narrow wooden boards, weathered a dark brown. The roof beams were enormously heavy and their ends, which could be seen under the projecting eaves, were beautifully carved. It was a fine, solid farmhouse and seemed to carry with ease the tremendous weight of the overhanging burden of snow.

Paolo came up to Werner.

'They say you saved my life,' he said gravely. The horror of his terrible experience still sounded in his voice.

'Oh, nonsense,' mumbled Werner, much embarrassed and staring over Paolo's head at the reflected light of the sunset, which turned the sky and clouds to rose colour above the blue-white peaks. The smoke from the houses curled comfortably upwards and the village lay protectingly round them.

'If my nonna found out she would hug you till you gasped for breath,' Paolo informed him.

'Who is your nonna?'

'My nonna, my nonna, my *nonna* – don't you even know that? She's my granny, of course, idiot! She's my father's mother and she's the grandmother of all her grandchildren, but she's lost them all except me. It's dreadful for her.' Paolo worked himself up till he was almost stamping on the hard snow. 'My granny would hug you a hundred times if she knew all you've done.'

'What have I done?' asked Werner, somewhat astonished.

'You . . . you . . . well, I don't know, actually,' answered Paolo, disconcerted. 'They might have told me that. They really might have told me that. But if they ever write one word,' his high, excited little voice became deep and threatening, 'one single word to my granny about what's happened, I'll . . . I'll . . .' His eyes flashed.

'That snow bath doesn't seem to have cooled you off much,' said Werner, looking down at him with dignity. He suddenly felt immensely superior to this queer little foreign boy. 'How old are you really?'

'You've asked me that before.'

'Well, you didn't tell me.'

At this moment Altschwank came out of the door, followed by a heavily built, elderly man with a heavy moustache and a short grey loden jacket. Altschwank beckoned to Mr Hutamäki.

'It's all right. Your party can sleep in the hayloft.'

'And the soup is on the table,' called Mr Taureggi, 'bean soup with pork.'

The boys came forward shyly. They muttered something and held out their hands. Taureggi shook them one after the other.

'The youngsters from the Pestalozzi village?' he said. 'I'm glad to see you. Come in. You may come from the four corners of the earth, but you're just the same young rascals as my own sons were. I can see that in your faces. In with you, hurry up, and shut the door or I shall get the stick from my wife. Welcome, welcome. And you're the foster father of these youngsters, so to speak?' He shook Mr Hutamäki's hand. 'Thanks for bringing them, Altschwank. Good night, and tell your wife to pack Werner into bed. He's shivering.'

It was true. The sun had gone. Everything was colourless

and grey and a little breeze blew like an icy draught down the village street. Werner felt suddenly cold to the very marrow. He glanced at the door which had closed on the others and turned away. He thought he could still hear Paolo's shrill voice.

'Come along,' said his father, and Werner felt a firm arm round his shoulders. At any other time he would have thought it silly, but now he felt thankful. His father's arm was strong and reliable, it even warmed him a little. Side by side, with their skis over their shoulders, they walked slowly together in the twilight along the narrow path between the snow-bound houses. Neither spoke.

Suddenly Werner was aware as he had never been before of the deep, warm affection which bound him to his father. He could not show it – he was as quiet and reserved as his parents. But he would never forget this walk with his father.

5

THE NIGHT IT HAPPENED

THE village settled down for the night in a fairly tranquil state of mind. The wireless had not announced any more disasters. The wind did not seem to be changing or freshening. The heavy snowfall everywhere had ended, and the masses of fresh snow on the most dangerous slopes seemed to be going to have a chance to settle in firmly. So although Urteli was one of the villages in the most dangerous area, the villagers went to sleep with quiet minds.

Finetti the butcher lay on his back with his mouth open, snoring. Perhaps he was dreaming that his son would come next day. Old John and his wife lay back to back under a heavy feather quilt; they slept lightly, as old people do, but when one or the other lay awake thinking, they kept still for each other's sake. Not that it helped much, for Mrs Rähmi's baby cried without stopping, and now and then they heard walking up and down. But towards midnight the baby stopped crying and the only sound was the creaking of the beams. The house is sighing under the weight of the snow, thought Old John.

Werner Altschwank lay in his little room next to the kitchen. He lay with his head under the dull red embroidered blanket, fast asleep. So he did not hear the soft crackling sound which came now and then from the logs that he had chopped and his mother had used to make up the great iron stove for the night. His father had bound up his leg with a wet bandage over a dressing of vinegar and fuller's earth. The pain had lessened at once and he slept like a log. In their room upstairs his parents lay in their wide double bed, talking about what had happened that afternoon and about the coming evacuation of the village.

Altschwank tried to comfort his wife. She would not hear of evacuation. 'I'd rather be buried under the snow!' she declared.

'You don't know what you're saying!'

'To go off and leave everything,' she mourned, 'every single thing we've got. What state shall we find it in when we get back?'

'With luck the danger may be over in a day or two,' he tried to calm her. 'Perhaps we shall be back in a week's time without anything having happened at all.'

'Then we shall have had all this trouble and wretchedness for nothing.'

'You're talking nonsense,' he said angrily and turned over in bed. But he was sorry. He knew she was not herself; the growing fear of the unknown masses of snow had weighed on the villagers day after day until some could bear it no longer. He turned over again to face her. 'Maria,' he said, 'you know what it means as well as I do. Houses and cowsheds can be rebuilt, but if people are killed, they're killed. That's why we've got to go. So as to save ourselves. Don't be so set against it.'

'You aren't coming yourself'; the voice beside him was jerky.

He took hold of her hand. 'It won't be two days before I come after you. We can't go off and leave the cows just like that. They're having to clear out of Glarmatt too. It all depends on transport. As soon as the cattle are shifted out of Glarmatt we shall move in.'

'Why can't you get Taureggi to take charge of our cows?'

'He'll have his hands full with his own cattle.'

'Do you know Aunt Augusta won't go unless she can take her three cats with her?'

'Let her take them,' said Altschwank. 'And let Werner help her. The more the boy has to do the easier things will be for him.'

'That's true of everyone,' said his wife.

40

'But more so of Werner. It's his only way of expressing himself.'

'I don't know what you mean,' she snapped.

'Most of us will learn more in the next few days than in all our lives before,' he said drily. 'Now let's go to sleep. We've a hard day before us. And let us pray God that the wind doesn't change, and that it doesn't thaw or rain or start snowing again. Then perhaps our village will be safe. Good night.'

His wife sighed. 'I wish I'd never come to live up here in the mountains!' she said bitterly.

'For shame, woman!' he exclaimed. 'Haven't we had some good years up here? Haven't we sometimes felt we were happier here in the mountains than we could be anywhere else in the world? Now and then they roar at us, it's true; maybe we shouldn't respect them if they didn't. Folk haven't much respect for anything these days. Believe me, it does one no harm to shake in one's shoes now and then. You should . . .' But he stopped suddenly because he could feel her shaking with suppressed sobs. 'Come here,' he said, putting his arms round her. 'We've had a good life together, and so we shall again. Things will come all right. I'm glad I brought you up here to live with me. There's nothing to beat the mountains even if they do now and then teach us a hard lesson.'

She did not answer but her sobs grew quieter. Presently they both fell asleep.

In his attic room in the café Bartel Gurtnelli pushed off his down quilt. He was dreaming that he had to shovel snow off a chessboard and that Old John kept sweeping it back with a huge broom. He flew into a rage and shouted 'Clear out!' but Old John only grinned and his mouth was suddenly full of brand-new shiny teeth. 'Get along with you!' Bartel shouted in his sleep. 'They're not real!'

In Taureggi's hayloft Paolo was talking in his sleep. He called for his granny and told her not to be afraid because he would come at once and help her. His voice sounded frightened. Mr Hutamäki, lying next to him in the hay, shook him by the shoulder to wake him. He could only understand the word 'nonna'.

'It's all right, Paolo,' he whispered in German. 'Everything's all right.'

'Yes. Why shouldn't it be all right?' asked Paolo's voice sleepily from the darkness.

'You were dreaming of your granny,' whispered Mr Hutamäki softly so as not to wake the other boys.

'Was I?' asked Paolo, astonished. 'Well, you may be right. Why shouldn't I?'

'Well, if you mean to do it again, don't make such a noise!' Mr Hutamäki advised him.

'Granny and I have been through all sorts of things together,' said Paolo.

There was a rustling in the hay and someone sighed. A cow moved with a clink of her chain. One of the boys snored softly.

'What a filthy row,' observed Paolo with disgust.

'Go to sleep,' said Mr Hutamäki. 'You can go on nattering tomorrow.'

'Nattering?' asked Paolo.

'Be quiet, Paolo, and go to sleep. Turn on your side and keep still.'

'Natter,' murmured Paolo, turning over obediently on to his side. 'Natter, chatter, smatter ... oh, I don't know ...' He rolled over on the other side. 'Mr Hutamäki, did *you* find it difficult to learn German?' he asked in a penetrating whisper.

Mr Hutamäki sighed. 'Paolo,' he said, '*go to sleep!*'

'Well, it was you waked me up,' came Paolo's voice reproachfully out of the darkness.

Mr Hutamäki could just see his face like a pale blob. 'You were having a nightmare. You were shouting and frightened.'

'I don't remember anything about it,' whispered Paolo

indignantly. 'Oh well, I don't mind,' he added graciously. 'You've been simply terrific these last few days.'

'Thank you,' said Mr Hutamäki as gravely as he could.

'I can hear you laughing,' whispered Paolo fiercely. 'That's silly, because I *mean* it.'

'We both mean well, Paolo. And now we're going to sleep. Good night.'

'Sleep soft, sleep sweet,' Paolo murmured. That came in a German song he had learned.

Mr Hutamäki did not answer. He heard Paolo mutter and grunt, heard him turn over and chuckle and curse. Then he gave a deep sigh, turned over again, another sigh, a contented little laugh, a sniff and at last – at last – there was silence.

'What a child!' murmured the elderly Finn with an amused smile as he turned over. But his last thought was about the next day's journey down to the valley. Would things go all right?

And then it happened. In the middle of the night. Just below the top of the Kühelihorn a great mass of snow broke loose with a crash like an explosion. Slowly it began to shift, it seemed to hesitate, but only for a little. A few seconds later the avalanche hurtled down, its path growing wider and wider, the force of the air driven before it blasting the village even before the thundering mass leapt upon the snow-covered houses and sheds like a wild beast, It lasted a far shorter time than anyone could have believed. One moment the village was safe and sound and fast asleep. The next, a great hole was torn in it. Part of it was still buried so deep in snow and wrapped in such deceptive silence that an onlooker would never have guessed the terrible thing that had happened. But part of it, even beyond the path of the avalanche, had houses blown down by blast, walls swept away, shutters and window frames ripped off and smashed. In an instant gaping black holes had been gashed in the white village and a white shroud of snow spread over its heart, just where Mr Baumgarten's office, the baker's shop and Gurtnelli's café stood clustered round the pump. The shattering blow which made everything that could split, burst, crack or smash fly to pieces with terrific force was followed by a minute or two of sinister silence. Then voices began to call. A woman screamed, one or two children cried, men's voices sounded harshly near at hand and further away. The alarm bell began to ring – a menacing sound above the stricken village. But it could not be Altschwank ringing the bell. His house lay buried.

Oil lamps were lit in houses here and there, light shone through cracks and through the patterns cut in the shutters. Men with lighted torches clambered over the shapeless mounds of snow, which were strewn with wreckage. More and more people started calling to each other. There was a sound of hysterical sobbing. Men shouted orders to each other. The dim beams of electric torches were pointed helplessly at the huge misshapen masses of snow from which protruded broken bits of wood, smashed crockery, the wheels of a pram, the leg of a chair, torn rags of stuff and ripped-off pieces of balcony. It was a chaotic sight which struck people speechless as they looked at it. One of them sobbed. Most of them stood about dumbly in the flickering light of the torches.

'The wind's changed,' said someone.

'Yes, the wind's changed,' someone else answered dully.

The changing wind, the falling snow, the towering mountains, high and pitiless, what can man do against them?

Man can build snow-breaks, he can put up wedge-shaped barriers at threatened points, he can dig trenches and plant trees, but once or twice in a century man is beaten.

The heart of the village had never been threatened in the memory of man. The villagers had feared for the outlying parts, where perhaps more houses had been built during the last few decades than was prudent in view of the known path of the avalanches. But they had taken all measures to ensure their safety.

The snow-breaks and fences, the barriers and trenches had all been under deep snow for days. The villagers had been anxious about the safety of the outlying houses, and with reason. But avalanches have sudden whims which leave one speechless with astonishment. The avalanche from the Kühelihorn had taken a totally unexpected route, one which it had never followed before. It had struck the centre of the village, the very place where people believed themselves safest: where Werner Altschwank and his parents lay asleep, where Bartel Gurtnelli was dreaming of a chessboard that he must clear of snow.

Then something amazing happened to Bartel. The blast picked him up and flung him, bed and all, away ahead of the avalanche, out through the torn and shattered roof which gaped like a strange black wound in the surrounding whiteness. He was flung so far that it was a quarter of an hour before he was found, still in bed, half smothered, his arm gashed by slivers of wood but otherwise unhurt. He was wrapped in blankets and taken to Taureggi's house, where a First Aid Post was set up; here the village midwife, who was also the district nurse, had her hands so full dealing with panic-stricken and hysterical villagers that she barely had time to get things ready to receive the injured.

Bartel was the sixth to be brought in. None of them were seriously injured but they had something in common all the time. All six of them lay on the floor in Taureggi's large sitting room, staring stupidly round them while they were given something hot to drink.

'I had such a quarrel with Old John,' muttered Bartel.

'Why, I've never done anything to you,' said Old John from where he lay in the darkest corner of the room. He raised his head, but let it fall back with a groan. His wife was sitting just behind him, bolt upright on a stool with her back against the wall, her hands folded in her lap.

'Lie still for a little while,' she said, 'it'll be better soon.'

'Of course,' said Old John. 'I only wanted to know what that boy has against me.'

His wife shrugged her shoulders.

Mrs Taureggi and her two grown-up daughters were helping the nurse, drawing out splinters and binding up cuts; there was a strong smell of iodine and ether. They ran out of bandages and had to tear sheets into strips instead. They worked away, fastening bandages, calming down their patients with a few quiet words, and sending out messengers to fetch the things they needed. Especially blankets, lots of blankets and quilts. And mattresses. The shock cases had to be kept warm. Even the sobbing women quieted down as soon as they were warm through and through.

Taureggi stood at the door and sternly drove away the people who would only get in the way, or who only wanted to ask him things he didn't know. Taureggi was always calm and people were not accustomed to his snapping at them, but they accepted it without surprise. Only Mrs Finetti, who came to him in tears to tell him that her pigs were buried under the snow, began to scream when he said roughly:

'Then go and dig them out, woman! You're not hurt yourself.'

'It's a man's work!' screamed Mrs Finetti. 'Digging is a man's work and you're just lounging there by the door . . .'

She got no further. Taureggi's muscular arm pushed her away and he shouted back: 'Yes, I have to stand here to keep donkeys like you from barging in and getting in everybody's way!'

But the real reason for his rage was that he could not be with the rescue squad. He was needed there too. Men kept on coming all the time to ask his advice and to fetch spades and other tools from his well-stocked shed. They could only get into it through a little window above the big doors, and even that was difficult. The big doors had been blocked with snow for the last four days. The rescue squad took away all the poles, slats, and sticks to use as sounding rods for prodding deep in the snow over the places where the victims were buried.

In Taureggi's cowshed, built against his house, everything was absolutely quiet. It was an oppressive quiet in which eleven boys tried to get dressed in the pitch darkness among the rustling hay. Antti's and Hans Peter's electric torches had burned out. After the first shattering crash in which every conceivable kind of noise was mingled, the dead silence was rather frightening to boys just jerked out of deep sleep. Then, when shouts and even screams came to them dimly, dulled by the great thickness of snow, many of them felt cold with fear. What had happened? An avalanche? And what about them? Could they get out of this cowshed? Mr Hutamäki's cigarette lighter brought relief. He lit one of the stable lanterns with it. The boys saw each other's faces, wide awake in the dim light. They saw the cows, stamping and jingling their chains restlessly, with little mumbling noises. They grinned at each other nervously and no one dared to say the word 'avalanche'.

'We'd better get dressed, boys,' said Mr Hutamäki.

They began to dress. Giuseppe and Nikolai were so excited that they started romping, and Giuseppe flung Nikolai back into the hay, but Mr Hutamäki called them to order immediately. At that moment the door of the cowshed was flung open and two men came in. They picked up the lanterns without a word and went out again.

'We'll manage,' Mr Hutamäki called after them.

'Yes, I thought you would,' said one of the men drily.

'What's happened?' asked Mr Hutamäki.

At that moment the alarm bell began to ring.

'An avalanche,' said the man. 'In the middle of the village.'

They were gone and so was the light. The cigarette lighter was no help. They were better without it. Their eyes would soon get accustomed to the dark. And besides, things could easily catch fire.

Mumbling to themselves, the boys dressed among the dry,

rustling hay. Suddenly one of the cows let out a frightened moo. Paolo began to laugh nervously.

'We'll be having a calf soon,' he giggled.

'Shut up, you ass!' snapped Giuseppe.

'I can't find my boots!' cried Jean Pierre.

'You've gone and put my trousers on, you clot!' Goldert complained to Martin. In their nervousness the boys each spoke in his own language. The effect was confusing. The cow lowed again. Clearly the cattle were restless.

'You often get two avalanches one after the other,' said Jussi, a Finnish boy, suddenly in sepulchral tones in German.

'Don't say such silly things!' Mr Hutamäki ordered him sternly in their own language, adding heartily in German for the benefit of the others: 'Nonsense!'

Somebody began to cry softly with dismal shaking sobs.

'Don't make a fuss, Paolo!' hissed Giuseppe.

An outburst of screaming was the answer.

'Shut up, Paolo!' It was Mr Hutamäki ordering him now. Paolo stammered something in Italian.

'He says he's frightened, sir,' Giuseppe translated.

'Frightened or no, crying won't help,' said Mr Hutamäki sharply.

The other boys had stopped talking.

'I won't be buried again! Not again!' shrieked Paolo suddenly. There was a sharp rustle and then the sound of a slap, presumably on a bare cheek. Paolo was suddenly quiet.

'I'm sorry,' came Hans Peter's voice, rather deeper than usual, 'but we can't have a squealing pig in here.'

'Hans Peter, don't take the law into your own hands like that,' said Mr Hutamäki. 'And Paolo, pull yourself together. There's no question of being buried. The avalanche has passed us and we haven't been hit. God help the poor wretches under the snow. As soon as you boys are ready we can go and help dig them out. So no more dawdling, mind.'

The boys finished dressing in silence.

6

UNDER THE SNOW

IN the first grey light of early morning the village looked even more cheerless than it had done at night in the orange glow of the torches.

During the night a courageous boy of 18, son of the Widow Bonza who kept the general shop, skied down to Glarmatt to carry the news of the disaster. Now, in the early morning, the first rescue party of troops arrived. Others would follow and the village was to be evacuated as soon as possible.

These first soldiers were heavily laden with gear. They were young men with red, earnest faces, who felt awkward at meeting the eyes of the stricken villagers. They brought a portable wireless transmitter-receiver with them. Contact with the outside world was re-established. The district nurse was relieved by medical orderlies.

No dead bodies had yet been recovered. There were thirteen people injured, two of them seriously. Five were still missing. These were the three Altschwanks and Mr and Mrs Gurtnelli.

The villagers who were searching in the heaps of snow with improvised sounding rods were relieved by the rescue party and placed under military orders. Taureggi, who had been in charge ever since Mr Hutamäki had come to take his place at the First Aid Post, joined forces with the officer, a young lieutenant with a tired, strained face and a thorough grasp of his job. While the soldiers screwed together their twenty-foot aluminium sounding rods and took up their position in two rows, Taureggi explained the local situation to the lieutenant.

When the sun came through the grey mist above the mountains like a glowing red ball and turned the western peaks above the valley to rose colour, the soldiers were standing in two long rows, prodding in the mass of snow many yards high and full of wreckage, stones and earth, which filled the centre of the village. They sounded carefully, keeping their long rods vertical and pushing them down, first beside the left foot, then in the space between their widely planted feet, then beside the right foot and then a short step in front. They hunted through the wreckage in a thoroughly systematic way.

Groups of villagers were digging, directed by Taureggi and a sergeant. The boys from the Pestalozzi village worked beside them with pale, tense faces, straight on without raising their eyes from their work. Werner, who had fetched them from the hut yesterday and had saved Paolo, lay somewhere under here with his father and mother.

'The whole upper storey must have been ripped off and smashed,' Antti heard someone say. 'Anyone sleeping downstairs will have more chance of getting out alive.'

What Antti had heard was true. Werner, who had been sleeping on the ground floor of the strong old house, was still alive. He crawled round among the wreckage like an ant that has lost its way, hardly knowing which way up he was, but pushing forward, driven by the blind urge for self-preservation, in the hope of finding the light.

He had been waked by a single crash and the hissing of something like a thunderbolt that whizzed past, singeing everything on its way. The noise of the crash seemed to consist of every kind of sound and to end in a shuddering jolt like the explosion of some mysterious firework, invisible in the blackness of the night. The whole thing seemed so unreal that at first he was not even frightened. He remembered only a feeling of immense surprise. Then the house began to tremble. And suddenly fear gripped him. The house shuddered and jerked and cracked as though it were being crushed and squeezed in some gigantic fist. Werner could not utter a sound. In a flash he thought of his father and mother asleep upstairs, but he could not move or call out. While the house was being crushed together with deafening cracks and rendings he lay in bed paralysed with fear. It all happened so quickly. The room began to sway, the walls caved in and split, the floor seemed to hump itself up in waves, and then suddenly everything was dark and still. There was no sign of the dim light from the little opening in the stove which his mother always left uncovered and which always cast a faint reflection through the open door and over the threshold of his little room. There was no more misty light from the night outside through the crack between the shutters. Not even a creak or a sigh from the broken woodwork. Only the silence and the blackness.

He felt round him with one arm. His hand knocked against a piece of a beam, close above his head. He groped further and felt splintered wood and frozen snow as hard as stone. Cold walls of ice where he had expected to find just a gap between the broken beam and crumpled wall. There was plenty of air. But for how long? And where were his mother and father?

He wriggled out of bed. He could not find the chair with his clothes on it at the foot of the bed, but he found his boots. These he managed to put on. There was no room to stand up. He tried, but only bruised and grazed himself.

He began to crawl, very slowly. Again and again when he bumped against a hard, cold wall of snow he had to grope round for another way out. There was no sound but his own panting and shuffling. He hardly felt cold at all. He did not feel the pain in his leg. He only felt afraid. He wanted to scream but he couldn't. His tongue and the roof of his mouth were dry. He swallowed again and again. He seemed to have too little saliva.

He was never thirsty in the night but now he was so terrified of thirst that he licked the snow when he came up against it. It was dirty, hard-packed snow with earth and grit in it. Werner spat it out. He felt he was going to cry, but he could not even do that. He could only push forward. On his tummy, because where he was now there was no room to crawl. Perhaps he ought to go back. But he did not know how. He did not know where he was. Was there still a kitchen, a cow-house, a cellar, a living room? Was it door frames that he bumped against? Were they doors that he wormed his way through or only holes? Would he never find an opening that was not blocked by the snow?

Slowly he began to realize how icy cold the snow walls around him were and how little protection his nightshirt and woollen under-pants gave. He smelled a smell of scorching. Did that mean he was near the stove and had the fire scorched anything else before the snow put it out?

He wriggled forward. His hands touched all sorts of things on the way. Broken pieces and things which he could not recognize by touch, and a saucepan lid and, yes, a slipper. It must be one of the old ones his mother wore in the kitchen. That was a comforting find. He left all the other things where they were but he took the slipper with him. He heard a soft ticking. It grew louder and louder. His hand touched something wooden. It was the kitchen cupboard, still standing upright with the alarm clock on top ticking away as if nothing had happened. He took the clock with him too, but a few minutes later he left it behind; the ticking was not soft any more, it seemed to bang against his cheek. He felt like flinging the thing into the darkness to be smashed against the snow walls that surrounded him, but he controlled himself and just put it down.

He went on with only the slipper. He had a feeling that he could walk here if he crouched low, but he didn't do it, for just then his fingers touched something small. It was a box of matches. Now at last a sound came from his throat and he was surprised to hear himself saying in quite a natural voice: 'What luck!'

He said it again deliberately: 'What luck!' That was right;

he wasn't mistaken. After that he said: 'It's cold.' That didn't sound so natural. It never entered his head to call: 'Mother! Dad! Where are you?' He knew in advance that it was hopeless.

He struck a match. His fingers were stiff with cold and he let the burning match fall. He struck another and held on to it tight. He lifted his arm and held up the weak little flame and looked round him. He did not recognize a thing. He saw a caved-in ceiling, broken beams, hay hanging down in hand-fuls through the holes. Cracked door frames, a door wrenched sideways and hanging ajar. Yes, he did recognize something. It must be the door from the wash-house into the cow-house. Above his head was the hayloft, or what was left of it. He could not get any farther and turned round.

He struck one match after another. He tried to find the passage, the stairs. If he could only get upstairs. There were only a few matches left. Now everything was so smashed up that he had to wriggle forward on his face. He did not know which way he was going. He could not recognize anything any more, till suddenly a stair-rail loomed up out of the snow in the light of the match. Perhaps he could get upstairs after all. He had lost his sense of direction so completely that he did not even know what was above him. The lumps of snow and bits of wreckage that he climbed over gave him nothing firm to hold on to. But he struggled on stubbornly. Again and again he found a way through, sometimes a very small one. Would he ever get to the top?

He used his last match and threw away the box. But he still had the slipper.

Now he caught himself muttering 'Mother! Dad!' foolishly and unthinkingly as he struggled forward. He shut his mouth firmly and stopped it.

'I won't give up,' he thought, 'I'll go on worming my way through everything, even if I go over the same bit twice. But I won't lie still.' And he wriggled a bit farther.

And then he saw light. It was very dim and grey, but he

saw it. And he heard voices. An order was shouted and he heard someone say:

'Not like that! This is the way to do it!'

'Nearly!' he thought. 'Just a little farther!'

Five minutes later they found him.

'We've found Werner Altschwank!' a voice shouted to someone down below. They were standing on top of a great pile of snow, part of which had been dug away. Werner crawled out of a hole.

'He's simply climbed out of the attic window!' called the same voice.

He felt himself being picked up and carried away. Then he was laid down somewhere and wrapped in blankets. They gave him something very hot to drink that made him glow inside and they said all sorts of things to him. He nodded and said he felt all right. Then he half dozed and didn't know much more. He felt himself being carried, it might have been on a stretcher, it was a nice springy feeling. The rough woollen blankets round him were not very warm. How long was it going to be?

Suddenly there was a face. Someone lifted the corner of the blanket and a boy grinned at him. It was Paolo. He took Werner by the shoulder, shook him and said:

'So you've not died of shock or starvation. Plenty of flesh on your bones.'

Werner could not help laughing.

'Why are you laughing?' asked Paolo. 'There's nothing to laugh at. This is a very serious business.'

'You're bats,' murmured Werner. He noticed how stiff his lips were when he tried to laugh.

'And you're barmy,' said Paolo in a hearty whisper. 'But don't go off with the idea that what happened to you is anything special. There's one of the men digging here who's been buried by an avalanche ten times.'

Werner said nothing.

'And there's an old lady – a funny old girl, very dark and with bandy legs – and she says her father was once flung 600 yards and didn't even get a cold in the head.'

'That's Aunt Augusta,' murmured Werner wearily.

The voice of one of the stretcher-bearers broke in sharply: 'That's quite enough. Leave the boy alone to rest now.' A man's hand with a uniform sleeve put back the blanket and tucked it carefully in round Werner.

'I was only just cheering him up!' he heard Paolo exclaim indignantly.

'I didn't ask the thing I wanted to,' thought Werner, 'whether they know what's happened to Mother and Dad.'

The search for the Altschwanks had not been abandoned, but practically nothing of the upper storey of the house seemed to be left when they found it under the snow. It was a miracle that Werner had found the opening formed by the staircase and managed to creep out into the light through the one remaining attic window which hung all askew in the snow, only just recognizable for what it was. Everyone had given up hope of finding Mr and Mrs Altschwank still alive. The Gurtnellis, however, had been found; they were not seriously hurt but suffering badly from shock. Even the news that Bartel had been found safe and sound after his amazing adventure could not calm them down. They were each given an injection and wrapped up extra warmly and pushed in between Bartel and Werner. Taureggi's big kitchen-living-room was getting very crowded.

The patients saw nothing of all the upset and preparations for the evacuation, nor of the feverish digging that went on all that night by torch-light. A second rescue squad arrived to relieve the first. The men were out on their feet. And still they had found no trace of Mr and Mrs Altschwank. The remains of their house had been dug partly free of snow; what was left was only a pitiful ruin. The three cows in the cow-house were dead; they had been flung on their sides by the weight of snow and smothered. Hardly anything was left of the furniture and belongings. A pathetic little pile of things had been set aside for Werner. There were battered saucepans, a few clothes, the clock, which had turned up again, some sodden bedding, broken chairs, the coffee mill with its handle gone.

'What will the boy do now?' the villagers asked each other, shaking their heads. They stood about in little groups, in the fitful glimmer of the torches which threw a flickering light over the salvage operations.

'He can come to us,' said Regli, the carpenter to whom Werner was apprenticed. 'He can have his keep and half-pay. We'll do our best for him.'

'Yes,' nodded the others. 'That's it.'

'He's a good boy, but quiet,' said Regli. 'You never know what he's thinking.'

'That's right,' the others agreed again. What else could they say? Regli was a good carpenter but he had a slut of a wife and was a bit short-tempered at times. Everyone knew that Altschwank had meant his son to go elsewhere later on. After a couple of years he might have gone to Glarmact as ski instructor. He had taken part regularly in ski-ing contests and come out very well. He and his father had studied English together in the evenings. The villagers had laughed about it among themselves more than once, but after all, Altschwank was the schoolmaster, even if his father had been only a peasant.

That night the snow began again. There was another bad weather report. So much snow fell in the early morning that further search for bodies had to be given up for the time being. But the village had to be evacuated just the same. The sappers had been making the route safe the previous afternoon and during the night. They had started off three small avalanches by letting off explosives.

Finetti's son had come up after all with his group, but he had been hit on the shoulder by a falling beam while helping to dig out the wreckage and now lay with his arm in splints among the other injured people waiting for transport down to the valley. He was a nice boy and was very much ashamed when his father flew into a rage by his bedside and called the officer commanding the rescue column every bad name he could lay his tongue to.

'Finetti, go back to your sausage making,' Old John muttered again wearily, and the phrase flew round the village to the great annoyance of the butcher, who considered himself a righteous man most unjustly treated by circumstances. He had managed to dig out his pig while it was still alive, but of course the creature had since died. His windows had been blown in and all his crockery and furniture smashed. Part of one side of his house had been ripped off and the doors burst from their hinges. But all people said to him was:

'Man, look at the Rähmis' house! It's been cut in half and half of it's lying in pieces on the other side of the stream! And just look at the Sturkis' and Miss Bonza's with their roofs stove in and the walls torn off! Man, go back to your sausage making!'

*

'I'll buy those three dead cows of Altschwank's,' said Finetti gruffly early on the morning of the evacuation. He would not go down himself till later when the cattle were driven down. For the present there was good business to be done with the troops, and on the pretext of providing them with meat he could stay behind with the villagers who had to look after their cattle.

'Will you pay a decent price for them?' asked Taureggi, who was looking after Werner's interests.

'Name it,' grunted Finetti.

Taureggi named a reasonable price. Finetti puffed out his cheeks and rolled his eyes skywards, but he agreed to it.

'I shall have to see Werner,' said Taureggi gravely. 'I'll tell him.'

Finetti looked after Taureggi as he walked away. The vigorous old man, who usually held himself so upright, now walked with tired, drooping shoulders as if he had suffered blow after blow. Finetti puffed out his cheeks.

'And what damage has *he* suffered?' he muttered scathingly. 'Not that much!' And he snapped his fingers. 'He just likes throwing his weight about because he happens to be the most important man in the village and feels that he's practically mayor!'

Finetti would never be able to understand how a man could worry about anything but himself and his own affairs. It never occurred to him that Taureggi was even then on his way to see Werner and tell him that he must give up all hope of ever seeing his parents alive.

On his way home Finetti met the Pestalozzi boys, who had been busy since early morning dragging heavy masses of snow on sledges to the stream outside the village. It was taken to the farther bank as well, great piles of useless snow dug out of the ruins and thrown into the swiftly running water which carried it all away.

Paolo was singing as he walked beside the empty sledge that they were dragging back.

'Is that the way to behave?' demanded Finetti. 'Aren't you ashamed?'

'It is a sad song, sir,' Paolo answered politely, 'a very sad song. I made it up myself.'

'And a saucy answer into the bargain!' shouted Finetti, beginning to get angry.

'He really means it,' another boy with a foreign accent said hastily.

'I made up that song on the death of a friend,' Paolo declared solemnly.

'Off with you!' yelled Finetti in a rage. 'Half the village plunged in mourning and you merely sing and get up to mischief.'

Paolo planted himself with firm dignity on his two small legs in front of the limping butcher. 'Sir,' he said earnestly, 'I don't think you have any feeling for music or that you have ever lost a good friend. If you had you'd know that what I say is true.'

Finetti felt just as if someone had shouted: 'Go back to your sausage making!' He turned away with a violent movement and hobbled on.

'And yet that man is really sad, I can see that,' said Paolo, looking after him solemnly. He had come off best in his exchange with Finetti but he was not feeling cock-a-hoop about it. He even waited a little before starting again on his sad little ditty. When he had finished, he said: 'It's a *very* pretty tune.' But he did not begin it again. And his friends, who knew him too well to jeer at him this time as they often did, said nothing either.

In silence the four boys pushed the big sledge along the narrow path through the ravaged village: Jussi, Holdert, François Mathieu and Paolo; a Finn, a German, an Alsatian and an Italian.

'I'm going to see Werner,' said Paolo suddenly. 'I'm not going to leave him alone now. I bet they've told him this morning about his father and mother.' And he went off.

The others ran after him. 'They won't let you in to see him.'

Paolo turned round. 'They will!' he called. 'I am my brother's keeper. I shall tell them so.'

And that was how Paolo came to Werner just after Taureggi had left him. Werner lay staring fixedly at the old, almost black beam of the roof. Paolo sat on the floor by the camp bed and began to stroke his hand softly, as one might stroke a cat. Werner said nothing, but he did not pull his hand away. Even Paolo said nothing. And that was the most that he could do for anyone.

7

EVACUATION

By eight o'clock everything was ready for the evacuation. Slowly the stream of people began to leave the village, silent and depressed, stared at by those who were staying behind.

Except for the escort of soldiers, who carried tiny children in their knapsacks or shouldered the luggage, the procession consisted mainly of women and children. Sadly the women moved away from their homes and village, where most of them left a husband looking after the cattle, shoring up houses and stables, and helping to dig out the ruins. Though the sappers were working their hardest to make the place safe, the women could not help feeling anxious. For although the Kühelihorn had shaken off its load of superfluous snow, how was the Glarbeckscher going to behave? The weather reports were no better than before and the sky seemed full of snow again.

The younger children, who found this journey much more fun than doing lessons, could not stop asking cheerfully when daddy was coming down with the cows and whether they would wait for him when they got down to the valley. Their mothers, with fear in their hearts, answered wearily and sometimes crossly.

'Who's cooking Daddy's dinner now?' asked a little girl of five in a shrill voice.

'They'll all get their meals from the cookhouse, darling,' said her mother, whisking away the tears with the corner of her black woollen scarf.

'Lovely grub!' said the lively voice of a young soldier who was trudging along behind them, carrying a hamper and an enormous brown paper parcel tied up with a great deal of

string. He had Mrs Rähmi's little boy on his back and the
child's fair head and red woollen cap were poking out of the
knapsack like a chicken out of an egg. 'Your daddy's never
had such lovely food to eat in his life,' the soldier went on,
'unless he's been in the Army, of course.'

Some of the women laughed shyly at this.

'After all, we're not at a funeral,' said one of them.

They were nearly all in black. They had black scarves tied
under their chins and had put on their Sunday coats, which
were black too. Some of them had put on coloured aprons
over their coats, because it was a pity to spoil one's best clothes
and you never knew what might happen.

They trudged on laboriously, mothers with children clinging to their hands, old people helped along by the soldiers,
groups of three or four children together trying not to show
how much they were enjoying it all.

'Down in Glarmatt we're going to get into a train! I've
never been in a train before!'

One soldier had a baby kid in his knapsack, another carried
a basket with three miaowing cats in it. They were Aunt
Augusta's cats, and Aunt Augusta hobbled along as best she
could beside her soldier, having flatly refused any further
help.

'You treat me as if I were an old crock!' she snapped. 'I'm
still quite steady on my pins and I've always got along all
right by myself and I'm going to now. Plenty of people need
helping more than I do. And now give me back my shopping
basket because if I lose sight of you I shall never see my things
again.'

However, there was no danger of losing sight of anyone.
The procession moved forward slowly and Aunt Augusta
could keep up quite easily. Perched on top of her head was a
wobbly black straw hat with a pink cotton rose that waggled
at each step of her black buttoned boots on the uneven
trampled snow. On either side rose a wall of snow, but here,

unlike the village, it was easy to see over it. Beyond the wall there was nothing to be seen but white peaks against a grey-white sky, white slopes with barely visible curves and creases; bushes, trees, and haystacks were all covered with a deep layer of snow which hid all the familiar landmarks from sight. Looking back, one could barely see the village lying a bit above them. Only the little church tower showed grey above the white hummocks where the roofs of the houses pushed up the thick blanket of snow. Even the little church tower had a cap of snow, incredibly thick and round.

Far below them lay Glarmatt. At this pace the journey would take at least three hours.

People who had skis with them carried them on their shoulders. The sick and the injured travelled on large flat military sledges, well fastened on with canvas and straps. Quite a lot of the villagers had brought sledges too. There were heavy sledges piled with baggage, crockery, bedding, cats, dogs and hens. There were sledges with the drivers perched behind, mostly little boys; the horses keeping their footing with difficulty on the slope. Old John and his wife sat in a sledge like this on top of a pile of bedding, pots and pans and a trunk of Mrs Rähmi's clothes. Old John's wife held Mrs Rähmi's baby in her arms and kept her eyes fixed on Urteli village on the hillside above them, the village which she had left only once in her life before, long ago, when she was a young girl and went to work in a hotel in Glarmatt.

Werner lay on a flat army sledge. The army sledges all glided one behind another in a closed column, two soldiers to each sledge. Werner would rather have walked; his leg was still a bit swollen, but nothing to speak of. The bandage his father had put on it earlier had been taken off and a new one put on. He had asked the medical orderly if he might keep the old bandage, without giving any reason. He had still got his mother's slipper with him under the blanket, and a purse with money that Taureggi had given him.

'There's more where that come from,' said the old farmer, 'but I'll keep it for you till you come back. Is that all right?'

Werner hardly realized that this was the money for the three dead cows. He knew that animals had been killed, he had heard a little girl crying about her goat. But it was all remote and seemed to have nothing to do with him. His thoughts wandered away after unimportant small things that had happened recently or during the past summer, to come back again always to his father and mother, who were still lying buried up there in the village, under the snow, between the walls of ice – he knew what it was like there. He was glad when the soldiers gave him something to eat or gave him a drink of hot soup – that helped. He was glad when Paolo came to walk by him, and the more nonsense Paolo talked the more it cheered Werner.

'That aunt of yours, Aunt Augusta or whatever her name is, the one with the three cats, she's a tough old girl!' Paolo informed him when they were half-way down. 'She marches along on her black bandy legs as if she were going to the end of the world. She's got a hole in her stocking – I bet she's left her darning wool behind!'

Werner smiled. He could see Aunt Augusta's legs climbing up her rickety ladder. And the new ladder that Dad had made for her. Dad – there it was again.

'There's one old boy,' Paolo went on, 'who's wearing three watches across his tummy and a hat on top of his woollen cap. He and his wife are carrying a basket between them full of chickens that are cackling like anything and making an awful row, but you can hardly hear it because the old boy and his wife are quarrelling like mad because they each say the other left the cock behind.'

Werner smiled again. He thought he knew who they were: probably his own master, Regli, and his wife. They were always quarrelling. Dad had said only the other day . . .

'And there's a boy who keeps teasing the little girls,' said

Paolo indignantly. 'If I catch him at it, I'll give it him! Teasing simply isn't *done* while you're being evacuated.'

Werner said nothing. He hoped Paolo would go on talking.

'I've warned him,' Paolo went on grimly. 'If I see you pulling a girl's hair one single time more, retribution will fall upon you. That's what I said to him,' said Paolo grandly. He flung out his chest and made himself broader than he was, but even so there wasn't much of him.

Werner lifted his head. 'I can't see where we are,' he said.

'Shall I sing you a song about thirty robbers who got lost in the mountains?' asked Paolo. 'I didn't make it up myself but it's quite nice.'

'Do you make up many songs?' asked Werner.

'Yes. I make up songs. I learned how to do it from my father. He wrote poems. He composed the most lovely poems all among the rubble after the air raid – that time when we were shut up in the cellar for three weeks. He scratched them on the stones. But afterwards we couldn't read them. It was a pity. But really, when we got out we didn't think of anything but getting something to eat.'

'How old were you then?' asked Werner. He was not really interested. He did not understand much of what Paolo was talking about.

'There you go again!' cried Paolo. 'Everyone always asks me how old I am! It's because I'm so small, they'll never believe so many things can have happened to me! That's the third time you've asked me,' he added indignantly.

This time Werner laughed. 'If you tell me, it'll be the last.'

'Are you some beastly official? Do you want to see my mother's marriage lines? Or to know where my father was born?' He stopped suddenly. That was twice he had mentioned his father. 'So long,' he said 'I'm going to see how the tail's getting on. Be seeing you.' And he trotted away again.

He had deposited his skis on one of the big sledges to have them out of the way. No one else would have been allowed to

go running about through the ranks like that, but Paolo
darted to and fro like a mouse through a hole, always with a
joke or a funny remark that disarmed everyone. He made the
most imploring faces, put on the most sympathetic airs and
managed to make everyone feel that he was a special friend.

'Paolo's at it again!' said Nikolai with an indulgent laugh.
'In a minute or two he'll start yelling again at something he
doesn't like.'

'Leave him alone,' said Jussi. 'He's bats, that's all.'

'But he's a decent little blighter, all the same,' answered
François.

They all liked Paolo though they found him tiresome now
and then.

'He's like a fly in warm weather,' said Antti slowly. 'It
buzzes round your nose till it drives you crazy, you try to swat
it but it keeps on coming back. And when you have a good
look at it you see how pretty it looks in the sun. Then it's off
somewhere else and suddenly everything's horrid and quiet
and not like summer any more.'

François laughed. 'Paolo must make us up a song about
that,' he cried, 'only he mustn't know it's him we mean. A
song about Antti's summer fly – a real Finnish fly that's missed
when it isn't there. Missed, I ask you! You can have it! I've
got enough flies sitting on the cheese at my uncle's in Marseilles.' François shook with laughter and the other boys
joined in.

Mr Hutamäki was keeping an eye on his boys, but he had
his hands full dealing with a whimpering village child that
was too tired to walk any further. He had been helping its
mother, carrying her two baskets. Now he handed them back
to her, gave his skis to Holdert, who had his own pair already,
and picked up the child.

'Only a little longer now,' he said to the tired mother, who
was stumbling along clumsily in her leaky shoes. He wanted to
ask 'Why didn't you put on stouter shoes?' but stopped him-

self. Urteli was a poor village. Perhaps those were the only shoes she had.

'When we get to Glarmatt,' he began, but the words died on his lips. Above them, far away, there was a dull rumble. 'There goes another,' he said, trying to speak as naturally as possible. 'But most of the avalanches coming down now aren't doing any damage,' he added.

'If only it's not the one from the Glarbeckscher,' said the young woman beside him.

The whole procession halted and stood still with pale, frightened faces. Had the village been struck a second time?

Silence again. But a minute or two later the alarm bell at Urteli began to ring for the second time in thirty-six hours. It was a sombre, terrifying sound in the white stillness in which no one spoke and each was full of his own fears.

'Carry on!' came the sharp order from the middle-aged sergeant in charge of the column of troops.

The sledges carrying the injured moved on again. The others followed unwillingly, but they had no choice. The soldiers in the rear urged them gently on. There was no point in standing still and getting into a panic. One old man who tried to turn back was prevented, gently but firmly.

Someone called: 'They'll send us news as soon as they can.'

People nodded. They tried to comfort themselves with the thought. But what was the good? Every man, woman and child was afraid for his own home, the women were afraid for their husbands, many were afraid for their cattle, the only valuable thing they owned, the thing they depended on for their living.

The man who had said they would get news soon was right. Barely a quarter of an hour later a figure on skis swooped down and caught up with the tired crowd of evacuees on foot. Everyone halted.

'No one hurt,' he told them, 'and the cattle are all right. But two of the houses have been hit.'

'Whose?' everyone wanted to know.

'Regli's, and Miss Altschwank's shop.' A murmur of sympathy went up from the crowd. Another Altschwank in trouble. But Aunt Augusta's voice was heard exclaiming shrilly:

'And who jeered at me for bringing my three cats with me? Now what have you got to say for yourselves?'

People laughed and looked embarrassed. Everyone was ready to help the old girl a bit and they were ashamed of themselves for making fun of her in the past; for they had, all of them, and not only because of her cats.

Mrs Regli broke down and sobbed. She dropped her basket of fowls and sat down limply on her bundle in the snow. Her husband tried to make her get up. 'There, there!' he said, and added to the neighbours standing round: 'I'll build my house up again all right.'

'That's it,' they said. 'We'll all give a hand.'

'I'm insured!' said Aunt Augusta triumphantly. 'Which of *you* has had the sense to insure your house?'

There was an indistinct murmur in reply. No one said 'Yes' or 'No'.

'They say there's been a relief fund opened for avalanche victims,' someone remarked. 'Half a million's come in, in less than two days. Perhaps we shall get everything back that we've lost.'

'Some hope!' said someone else.

'And what about the lives lost?' asked a third.

'Forward march!' ordered the sergeant.

Bartel Gurtnelli was walking quietly behind the sledge on which his parents lay. His mother was sobbing and his father's eyes were shut. He did not answer when anyone spoke to him.

Bartel slipped round to the side of the sledge and bent over his father as he walked along. 'Dad,' he said softly, 'Dad, you're insured too, aren't you?'

His father did not answer.

'Dad, then we'll be able to build everything up again.'

Gurtnelli's café was gone. Not a wall was left standing. The hard-packed masses of snow, heavy as lead, had crushed what was left of the house like a crumpled matchbox, hours after the avalanche had come to a stop.

One of the medical orderlies caught Bartel by the sleeve. 'Let your father rest. He's suffering from shock. He'll be all right again. It'll take a couple of days.'

They had nearly reached Glarmatt by now. People came out to meet them, some on skis and some on foot. There were inquisitive winter sports tourists, too, who had not been able to get away yet and who wanted to get a close-up view of this evacuation of a whole village. Where the first houses began a man stood filming the weary procession. One old man pulled his hat right down to his eyes and two women put their hands in front of their faces.

'For shame, young man!' said Aunt Augusta in her most penetrating voice. 'Do you want to put pictures of our people with their eyes all swollen with crying in your nasty newspaper? Is that what you're paid for? Well, look at me, then! I've cried more than any of them when I was young!' and she planted herself close up in front of the lens so that he could not take a photo at all.

The man retreated behind a wall of snow and set up his camera again at a distance.

'That's better!' called Aunt Augusta. 'You can come and learn manners up in our village.'

Paolo appeared beside her. He stared at her in deepest interest and kept beside her when she plodded on again. She glanced at him as if he were a black beetle.

'Is it true?' he asked. 'Have you had a lot of troubles?'

The old woman looked at him but said nothing. She folded her lips together tightly in a way that would have silenced anyone else. But not Paolo.

'So have I,' he said. 'I have had a lot of trouble, and so had my granny. You're a bit like my granny. You're fierce like her. But I dare say you have a kind heart, like she had. That will be interesting.'

'What will be interesting, young man?' snapped Aunt Augusta.

'Well, I shall keep an eye on you to see if I'm right,' said Paolo, but he gave her such a disarming look that instead of being angry she blinked at him. He saw that her eyes were red and watering.

'Is something the matter with your eyes?' he asked.

'The light hurts them,' she said. She passed her old hand over her inflamed eyes. 'And my spectacles got broken last night when it happened.' She spoke more softly than before, almost naturally. She was not accustomed to other people taking an interest in her welfare.

'If you buy a newspaper I'll read it aloud to you this evening,' offered Paolo unexpectedly. He spoke eagerly, he was mad on newspapers. 'Do you like fires and train smashes and strip cartoons?' he asked.

'Strip cartoons? What sort of things are they?' asked Aunt Augusta suspiciously.

'Oh, they're stories with strong men in them, great big strong men,' said Paolo dreamily. He looked up at her wrinkled face. 'But perhaps you're not frightfully interested in strong men? Or nice murders?'

A sudden idea seemed to strike the old woman. 'Where's that soldier?' she demanded at the top of her voice. 'Where are my cats?'

'I'll go and find them,' said Paolo and was gone.

The soldier with the cats was walking less than ten yards behind them. He now carried a little boy on his back as well, a pale, grave child who had put on the soldier's cap and was now clinging tightly to his protector's thick sandy hair. Every time the little boy turned round to see if his mother was keeping close behind, the soldier made a face. But he said nothing. They were there now.

8

PAOLO AND WERNER

EVERYONE was glad to get to Glarmatt. They had a hearty welcome there. More and more people came running to meet them, and saucepans of hot soup and jugs of steaming coffee were brought out of the first houses as they reached them. They were surprised at the warmth of their welcome but even more astonished at what they saw.

Glarmatt was a flourishing tourist village, larger than Urteli, and they had known that it would be as deep in snow as their own home. The houses were sunk in snow right up to the first floor, the whole look of the place was altered, the fat white cushions on the roofs elbowed each other from house to house, and the little alleys between were dark or filled with snow. But they had not known that no fewer than three avalanches had come down on it the night before; they had not expected to find the place swarming with soldiers busy digging for people buried under the wreckage. The largest hotel had simply been swept away; it had vanished under the snow. All this upset the newcomers and filled them with terror.

'Is it the same everywhere?' they asked anxiously.

'No. Not everywhere. But here near you and in Rohstocker-alp and in Bels it's like this,' they were told. 'It's worse in this part of the Alps. We've all got to leave. Extra trains down to the valley are to be put on tomorrow. But the line to Brachen was blocked again yesterday. We've got to wait.'

People stood about in patient little groups in front of the mayor's house. Commands were shouted to the troops. Officers strode to and fro, and so did busy, worried-looking civilians. Some of them had white bands round their arms, others a band with a red cross. No one knew exactly what was to be done with the evacuees from Urteli or where they were to be housed until more transport arrived. The Three Kings Hotel had offered to put up twenty people; many of the tourists had gone and those who were left seemed willing to put up with anything in order to help. The Golden Lion could take fifteen. Then there were the station waiting rooms, but someone said they were full already.

Still, it was a good idea to be at the station in case the line were suddenly signalled clear and a train left. The sooner one could get away from here the better.

Mr Hutamäki called his boys together.

'We're going to the station,' he said. 'We'll camp there till a train goes.'

'I won't move from here without Werner,' declared Paolo. The other boys backed him up.

'But Werner's being looked after by the Red Cross,' objected Mr Hutamäki.

'He doesn't need to lie on a sledge,' said Paolo. 'He'd much rather walk. He said so.'

But the point soon settled itself. All the sledges were being taken to the station so that the injured could be sent down straight away as soon as a train left. There was a hospital at Brachen. And it was safe there.

More than half the people from Urteli trooped off along the road to the station. It lay a little beyond the village, near the barracks, which were built just outside.

Glarmatt was not looking like itself at all. There was no sign of the usual brightly coloured throng of tourists in the village street. The foreigners who were still there were helping to clear the wreckage.

Four English boys were pushing along a heavy sledge piled with snow towards the bridge, to shoot the lumps of snow into the river, just as the boys from the Pestalozzi village had done the day before up at Urteli. Hundreds of men, soldiers and civilians, were sounding and digging away at the huge heaps of snow which stood as high as houses. Avalanches had hit the village from three sides and left it looking as desolate as Urteli. The only difference was that the snow was dirtier here and more trees had come down with it. Their shattered trunks stuck up out of the mass of snow and rubble and earth. The fresh wood where they had been snapped off, or ripped and torn, smelled strongly of resin.

Whole walls had been carried away. A staircase stood up in the air swaying crazily. A bed lay in the snow. Above it a wash-basin dangled by its pipes from a broken wall. Shreds of wallpaper hung down limply. The telephone wires were a tangled mass, the posts snapped off, the lines dead.

Twenty-three animals of all sizes had been buried by the snow so far. Seven people were missing. The sick bay at the barracks was so crowded with the injured that there was no room for any more.

The further the villagers from Urteli walked through the village the more clearly they saw that Glarmatt had no room to offer them. The undamaged houses and the barracks had given up all the space they could spare to their own villagers. Glarmatt itself was waiting to be evacuated. Everything depended on transport. Half-way to Brachen another avalanche had fallen on the line. There was even a rumour that a snow-plough had been sent from Arth Goldau to clear that part of the line. But what next? There might be another avalanche at any moment.

They passed the shops. Steep steps had been cut in the snow down to their doorways below. Narrow passages had been dug round nearly all the houses, but even so there was next to nothing to be seen of the shop windows. A few shop signs – in English and German because of the tourists – were still legible. But most of the show-cases were empty and the windows had been boarded up with heavy planks to save them from being damaged by the weight of the snow. Near the dance hall a board stuck out of the snow with a red arrow on it pointing to the skating rink where the band used to play.

The trampled path through the village had been dug wider here than in Urteli, which was a much smaller place, but when two ox-drawn sledges came along they had each to hug the wall of snow. The oxen wore bells round their necks. Their white coats with pale brown patches looked dirty against the shining whiteness of the snow. The small dark men with stubbly chins who drove the oxen made shrill noises in their throats to urge their slowly moving beasts forward, but it did not help much. Slowly the sledges slid past; the first one was filled with coal, the second with onions, oranges and cabbages. For one reason or another the evacuees stood staring after the sledges a long time.

At the end of the street, at the foot of the dozen steep snow steps in front of her newspaper and cigarette shop, a small, grey-haired lady, whose eyes were watering behind her spectacles, stood and looked at the procession of refugees.

'Look! we can buy a newspaper there, Miss Augusta!' cried Paolo and sprang down the slippery steps at such a speed that the little old lady put her hands over her mouth in a fright.

The latest newspaper was the day before yesterday's and Paolo got it for nothing; also cigarettes, ten packets of them, and stuffed his pockets full.

'Not for you, young man,' said the old lady, looking at him rather severely. 'You're too young. Divide them among the poor things who need them.'

Paolo suddenly stared at her spectacles, fascinated, as if he would stare them off her nose.

'My old granny has lost her spectacles,' he began pathetically. 'You haven't – you wouldn't have a pair to spare?'

The old lady shook her head with a smile.

'I'm afraid my glasses wouldn't be right for your granny, my dear,' she said.

'And she's lost her house and her shop as well,' Paolo took up the sorrowful tale. 'We don't know how we're going to live at all when we get back.' He gave a half sob. By now he really believed what he was saying. 'We've nothing left but three cats. And cats eat an awful lot. And when you haven't any spectacles everything's more difficult still.'

'If you walk back a little way you'll find the optician's shop on your right,' said the old lady kindly. 'He is a good man. Perhaps he can do something for your granny.'

Paolo was off and away before the words were out of her mouth. He found the optician's quite easily.

'To think I never thought of it before!' he scolded himself. 'What an ass I am!'

He pranced into the shop confidently enough. The bell on the door tinkled and the optician came out from behind the counter in his white coat as if there were no avalanches in the neighbourhood. But none of Paolo's hard luck stories did any good. The optician was not going to prescribe glasses for someone whom he had not seen.

'Haven't you ever heard of different kinds of lenses, young man?' he asked, 'a bright boy like you?'

'Then I'll bring her here!' cried Paolo excitedly. 'Then you can see her for yourself. But without her glasses she might break her legs coming down those beastly steps of yours.'

'If your grandmother wants a pair of glasses she'll have to come here for them,' answered the optician unmoved.

'But—' began Paolo.

The optician looked at him over his glasses. Then he raised his eyebrows, smoothed the lapels of his white coat, retired once more behind his table of instruments, sat down and left Paolo to his fate.

Paolo slunk away with his tail between his legs. However, a moment later he stuck his head in at the door and, while the little bell was tinkling, he said with a beaming smile:

'Cheerio, then! I'll be back with her in a quarter of an hour.'

He rushed to the station as fast as his legs would carry him. Mr Hutamäki would probably scold him for lagging behind.

The party of villagers from Urteli were at the station already. They stood huddled together in a gloomy, depressed-looking group on the small platform that was crowded with other travellers. The station staff, consisting of five men, went to and fro among the waiting people and tried to calm them. Yes, certainly there were two trains waiting there. One of them was a relief train which would leave as soon as word came through that the line was clear. No, it was not one avalanche blocking the Glarmatt-Brachen line, but three. More and more men had been sent by the railway company to help with the work of clearing the line. There were a couple of hundred working on it now, and a second snow-plough had been sent to help clear things up. The troops were helping too. But the work was tricky. It kept being held up by the danger of further falls. Railway engineers and avalanche experts were in charge. The public must be patient.

No, they could not go into the waiting rooms, those were for the injured. Other people must wait on the platform. The small station restaurant was crammed full of tourists waiting for a train to take them home, there was no room there. No, no one might go into the signalbox except the signalmen.

Paolo pushed his way through the crowd, stumbling over every kind of box and bundle and smiling disarmingly whenever anyone scowled at him. He enjoyed the crush and bustle and the buzz of voices. He liked being among people. He felt happiest in a crowd, provided he was not hemmed in too tightly to move.

The villagers from Urteli made a quiet, patient little group among the other people. They were strangers here. They felt unhappy and forlorn now that the soldiers who had brought them down from the village had gone. There were just two medical orderlies left to look after the injured.

To his great delight Paolo discovered Werner with Aunt Augusta. Werner was leaning against a post and staring gloomily in front of him.

'Miss Augusta, you must come with me,' said Paolo firmly. 'I've found a pair of glasses for you.' He glanced triumphantly at Werner. 'I've been to see the spectacle man. Everyone wants to help the poor evacuees,' he went on, putting on his most pitiful expression. But if he had expected applause he was disappointed. Werner did not move a muscle.

Miss Augusta looked at him suspiciously. She could not get accustomed to the idea that a strange small boy wanted to do her a good turn.

'Come along!' cried Paolo impatiently. 'The spectacle man's waiting for you!'

Werner stayed behind.

On the way Paolo tried to make Miss Augusta understand the part she was to play. She was his granny, she had lost her house and her shop, her children and her grandchildren – nine of them. 'It's all quite true,' he assured her with conviction. 'You've only to imagine that you *are* my granny. Only that bit about the cats – no, that *wasn't* true.' He was so frank in the way he mixed up truth and falsehood that he had Aunt Augusta quite bewildered.

When they came back to Werner she had a much finer pair of spectacles than she had ever owned before.

'And it didn't cost a ha'penny!' Paolo announced delightedly.

'I shall pay him later,' said Aunt Augusta with dignity.

Paolo gave a disparaging sniff. 'Don't you chuck away the gifts of the Almighty like a blasted –'

'Of the optician, you mean,' snapped Aunt Augusta. 'And blasted isn't a nice word for a child to use.'

'I have my own vocabulary,' said Paolo loftily.

Werner had not uttered a word all this while. Now, with a face stiff with indignation, he said:

'I've no use for boasting and I've no use for begging and lying.'

Paolo stared at him for a moment, staggered. Tears of rage rushed into his eyes and he began to shriek abuse.

'You horrible, beastly prig of a village boy – you think you know everything, don't you? *You've* never gone hungry. You've never seen your brothers and sisters die. You've never slept in a ditch by the roadside or seen a man shot dead. *Your* village has never been bombed. You – you – you – *you* haven't got a granny like mine! She hasn't a tooth in her head, but her muscles are like a ship's cables and her eyes are like thunder and lightning. And I was the only one she was able to save – do you understand that, you clot? *Me!* All the rest were killed. In the war. The war that you silly, pampered blighters didn't have here. You – you – *you've* never been buried in a cellar with nothing to eat but a bit of mouldy bread and a few rotten carrots. You don't approve of begging and lying, don't you? You've never been crazy with hunger and fear like a cat caught in a trap. You belong in an eagle's nest, you do, not among real people, you stuffed dummy, you!'

Paolo shrieked himself hoarse. Werner stood quite still beside him. His face was crimson. He did not seem to hear. The people in the crowd round them listened in astonishment. A man caught Paolo by the arm.

'See here, youngster –'

Paolo snatched his arm away. 'Leave me alone!'

Mr Hutamäki pushed his way through the crowd, towering a head and shoulders above them. He looked worried. Hans Peter and Antti followed close at his heels. But before they reached the excited little Italian boy, Werner gripped his arm like a vice and hissed fiercely:

'Stow it! Or I'll pinch your arm black and blue!'

Paolo gave a gasp. 'I thought you were a decent chap,' he panted, 'but you're nothing but a great big bully, you!'

Werner's grip tightened. Paolo kept his mouth shut. Tears streamed down his face, not tears of pain but tears of rage.

Mr Hutamäki shouldered his way to their side. He looked down at Paolo grimly. Paolo blinked.

'You know what you promised before I'd let you come

with us,' said Mr Hutamäki severely. 'You promised not to make scenes, and now you're doing it here of all places.' He glanced round, indicating the pale, anxious, closely packed crowds of waiting people. 'As if things weren't difficult enough already,' he added. 'And *you* know what it's like to be a refugee,' his voice was softer now. 'Come along.' He took Paolo's arm and led him quietly back to the other boys.

'We'll keep together now. Then you won't go racing round like a dog without a collar.'

Paolo hung his head and followed him.

Werner stood looking after them.

Paolo looked over his shoulder. They stared at each other. Werner felt Aunt Augusta's bony hand on his arm.

'These spectacles do make a wonderful difference,' she said in a voice which he hardly recognized.

Werner's stern expression relaxed a little, but Paolo was too far away to see. He was standing at the other end of the platform with the other boys, talking away with quick gestures of his little hands. Werner felt rather out of it.

Suddenly everyone jumped. A booming voice sounded over the loud speaker that had been rigged up in the station. The words were repeated twice before the waiting crowds grasped their meaning. There would be no train that afternoon. Passengers were asked to move quietly into the waiting rooms. The injured had now been removed to the station master's house. Those people who intended to spend the night in the waiting rooms instead of trying to find a bed in the village were begged to behave in an orderly manner and to try to fit in with each other. 'We expect the regular train service to start running again early tomorrow morning, as well as several relief trains,' the booming voice ended.

The doors of the waiting rooms were opened and people surged in past the station officials. It was nice and warm inside and there was more room than one would have expected. Little groups of people trickled back to the village carrying their baggage. In the end everyone who wanted to stay in the waiting rooms found room to lie or at least to sit down.

Swallowing his pride and annoyed with himself for doing it, Werner manoeuvred for position till he found a place for himself and Aunt Augusta not far from the Pestalozzi boys. Aunt Augusta sat on the bench with her shopping bag and her cat basket by her feet. The cats were quiet now. Werner sat on the floor and leaned against the wall, staring straight in front of him. After a time he could not keep it up any longer, and he let his eyes rove about till they found Paolo. Then he saw that Paolo had been sitting waiting for him to do just that. He looked at Werner hopefully and gave him an enormous wink. Werner felt himself grow hot all over and looked away again. 'I'm absolutely bats,' he thought.

A trolley was wheeled round with thick soup for the evacuees and slices of bread to go with it. Those who liked could go into the village and buy provisions there.

Aunt Augusta gave her soup to the cats. She took them out of their basket one by one and gave each of them a turn at it. They were frightened and difficult to handle, but she refused to let Werner help her.

When it began to get dark, someone brought two lighted hurricane lanterns with red glass and hung them on a couple of nails in the wall. The dim, rosy light shone down on the untidy crowd of waiting people. Some of them had fallen asleep huddled against the piles of luggage, exhausted by everything that had happened in the last couple of days. One little girl was crying. Most of the children sat leaning wearily against their mothers, staring at nothing in particular. One or two babies were being suckled by their mothers and gurgling contentedly. A few men's voices made a deep note as they talked. Women whispered together. Hardly anyone showed signs of impatience.

But as the evening wore on, things grew more difficult. Aunt Augusta's cats began to miaow stridently. Two dogs that were fastened outside began to yelp. A baby started howling. Children kept on asking their mothers questions and were answered in a repressive whisper.

A little red-haired English girl was sitting next to Werner. She was with her father, who was a major, and they had turned up after the others. They were among the very few tourists in the waiting room; most of them were spending the night in the restaurant or had given up hope of getting away by the first train and gone back to their hotels.

The English girl kept doing endless sums on her fingers. After that she played some kind of game with her father, but Werner couldn't make head or tail of it. Her name was Winifred and she called her father 'Daddy'. Werner tried to understand something of what they said. He thought of all the evenings he had spent at home learning English with his father by the light of the paraffin lamp, with Mother pouring out coffee. . . . He still had her slipper stuck in his belt. Perhaps later on they would find more things belonging to his home. But would they keep everything?

He felt himself growing drowsy. That was a good thing. He did not want to think too much. Paolo did not think much either, he chattered nineteen to the dozen instead. And yet. . . .

Werner moved. His leg hurt. Winifred nudged him. 'I say, can you speak any English?' she asked, but shyness overcame him and he shook his head. She smiled at him and he tried to smile back, but it was not much of a success. He was thoroughly fed up with himself.

Aunt Augusta had nodded off to sleep. Werner stood up, picked up the basket of cats and carried it outside, stumbling over legs and bodies on the way. Outside in the dark he put the basket down on the platform and carefully undid the lid. The cats spat at him. The straw they were lying in was awfully smelly. Their eyes shone green in the darkness and one of them tried to jump out. He shut the basket again quickly, feeling rather helpless. It was horrid to leave them in the dirty straw.

The door of the waiting room creaked behind him and he looked round. It was Paolo.

'I've been a perfect swine,' said Paolo, 'but I was in such a rage.' Werner did not answer. He wanted to say something, but he couldn't think of anything to say.

Paolo looked from him to the basket of cats.

'I saw a heap of straw,' he said, 'away over there, where the cattle trucks are. Come along.' They picked up the basket between them.

While they were walking along Werner said as casually as he could:

'Aunt Augusta's awfully pleased with her glasses.'

The cats miaowed again plaintively. At the end of the covered platform was a mountain of straw, covered with snow on the windward side. Two empty cattle trucks with the doors open stood near by.

'If we shut the doors carefully, we can let them out for a bit in one of the trucks,' said Paolo.

They climbed in, shut the doors and opened the basket in the darkness. The cats jumped out with a wild rush. They ran about in the rustling straw on the floor of the truck but went on miaowing. The two boys could not see each other in the dark. There were only the green, gleaming eyes of the cats and the narrow strips of dim light which came through the crack of the door, and from somewhere high up in one corner, where there must be a ventilator.

'They try to teach me not to tell lies at school too,' said Paolo suddenly, 'but I simply can't see the point.'

It took Werner quite a time to think up an answer to this.

'If you'd told the truth you'd still have got the glasses just the same,' he said. But there was a lot more that he wanted to say, only he could not find the right words.

'Shucks,' said Paolo, 'I'm not so sure of that. And anyway it wouldn't have been nearly so exciting.'

'If you can't get by without lying it's just like not being able to walk without crutches,' said Werner with some difficulty.

'What's wrong with crutches if you're a cripple?' demanded Paolo hotly.

'That's quite different,' Werner retorted. 'A cripple can't get along without crutches. But if you use lies as crutches it's because you're lazy, or because you like having the other fellow on, or because you're afraid.' He was thankful for the darkness. He knew he could never have said all this if it had been light.

'And how d'you know I'm not afraid. Sometimes. Or – oh, blast you,' Paolo burst out. 'I think you're barmy and you don't understand *a thing*, but you're not a bad sort of blighter really. Though I'm sure I don't know why I like you.'

Werner said nothing. He was hurt and puzzled.

Their eyes had grown accustomed to the darkness by now and they could vaguely make out each other's shape. They could not distinguish faces. The cats had quieted down. Now and then the straw rustled.

'It's going to be a job to catch them again,' said Paolo. 'Have you got any matches?'

'No,' Werner answered. And suddenly all the crushing fear of being buried gripped him again, his terror among the hard, icy walls of packed snow, the smashed beams and broken fragments of the house. Matches. It was absurd but he probably owed his life to that box of matches. He was suddenly very glad.

'Are you glad you're still alive?' he asked Paolo, thinking of all the Italian boy's war adventures.

'Glad I'm alive?' repeated Paolo incredulously. 'Why, I think it's simply smashing! It was a terrific stroke of luck for all of us, being sent to the Pestalozzi village. You bet I'm glad! Just think of all the exciting things I'd have missed!'

'You wouldn't have known,' said Werner.

'No, but I know *now*. And my granny – just think what it would be like for my granny if she had no one left at all.' Now he'll start howling again, thought Werner; however, Paolo didn't howl. Instead he began to laugh. 'Though I dare say she'd have got on all right without me if she had to,' he chuckled. 'Give her a sunny place to sit in and a bit of wall to lean against and she flourishes like a weed!' He laughed contentedly in the darkness.

'You're lucky to have her still,' said Werner quietly. 'And you're lucky to live in the Pestalozzi village.'

'Haven't you any one left now?' asked Paolo carefully.

'Only Aunt Augusta and an uncle and aunt that I don't know in Zurich. Mr Taureggi says I can live with him for the present.'

'That's nice of him,' said Paolo.

Werner did not answer. Presently he said: 'Shall we catch the cats now and put them back in their basket?'

'Oh, you simply must listen to this first!' cried Paolo, catching Werner by the arm, and he began to sing. It was a queer, monotonous tune with sudden outbursts of high notes here and there. The words sounded as if he were making them up as he went along, but he must have thought them out before.

It was a song about all the things that life is full of: funny things and sad things and jolly things that make you want to burst out singing. The sudden pleasure when a stranger smiles at you in a crowded street, or you hear a cock crow joyfully at daybreak. The gentle, quiet things like a new-born lamb or the warm sunshine. The joy that fills you when you hear a man singing in a shadowy barn, comforting you for everything that has gone wrong and making your heart leap with joy at being alive, just like the cock at daybreak.

'H'm,' said Werner, rather embarrassed. He was glad Paolo had let go of his arm.

There was a knock on the side of the truck. 'Oy!' shouted

a voice outside Someone pushed open the doors and a railway man flashed the light of a hurricane lantern into the truck. 'What's all this?' he asked. 'Are you giving a concert in here in the middle of the night?'

'Look out!' yelled Paolo. 'Our cats!'

One of them had already leapt for the doors. Paolo slammed them in the man's face while Werner grabbed the cat. It was a near thing.

'If you'll come in *carefully* you can help us,' called Paolo. 'We can't see a thing in here.'

Five minutes later they were walking back along the platform towards the warm waiting room, with the cats once more safely in the basket with some nice clean straw. It was only now that the boys noticed how cold they were.

'You give me those cats and I'll stick them in the parcels office,' said the man.

'My granny would have a fit if you did that!' exclaimed Paolo indignantly. 'She's lost everything in the world except her cats, *everything*, I tell you!'

'Everything?' asked the man, startled.

'Every single thing!' said Paolo dramatically, 'her house, her shop, her children and grandchildren – seven of them – her –'

'All right, you can keep the cats,' said the man hastily and walked quickly away.

Paolo put out his hand to open the waiting room door but Werner held him back. Paolo looked up at him in surprise. In the dim blue light on the covered platform his eyes looked unnaturally large and black.

'I shall think about it,' muttered Werner.

'About what?' asked Paolo, astonished.

'Oh, you know – all those things you were singing about.'

'Oh, yes, there are lots of things like that,' said Paolo carelessly and opened the door of the waiting room.

The warm fug struck them in the face. It smelled sour and

stuffy. Werner shrank back but Paolo couldn't care less. They picked their way back carefully to their places in the dim light of the lanterns on the wall.

The English girl had fallen asleep against her father's shoulder. Werner sat down carefully beside her. Aunt Augusta did not notice anything. She had dropped asleep where she sat, muttering a little and now and then jerking her head as if something had startled her. Most of the people were asleep or looked as if they were.

Werner looked round slowly. He felt that in some queer way he was linked with all these people, not only the people from his own village, but the English girl with her father and the three soldiers on the other side of the room. There were so many people that he didn't know at all and yet he had this odd feeling of being one with them. A feeling of belonging together. It was funny – but was that one of the things Paolo had meant in his song? The sudden pleasure when a stranger smiles at you in a crowded street? No one was smiling here. And yet –

He leaned back against the wall with his hands clasped round his knees. He shut his eyes and thought: 'I wish I could cry.'

9

THE TRAIN JOURNEY

To everyone's surprise the early morning train left punctually. The relief train was to follow. It seemed a miracle that the line was signalled clear, for it had been snowing all night, not heavily but without stopping.

'I should think this train is the only one today that will leave according to the time-table,' observed a gloomy old gentleman who came and sat down in a corner seat by the window next to Mr Hutamäki.

It was a very little train that they were in. Only five coaches were hooked on behind the engine. Three of them were for passengers, each with two double compartments on either side of a luggage van. Behind these came two cattle trucks. Frightened cattle were hastily loaded into them with anguished lowing.

Passenger carriages and luggage vans were filled to bursting point. Two of the luggage vans were filled with stretcher cases, lying tightly packed side by side. The walking wounded, including Finetti's son with his broken arm and the three soldiers who had sat opposite Werner in the waiting room, had seats in the carriages. People were packed together like sardines. The boys from the children's village sat three deep on each other's knees, joking and larking about. Werner was shyly rocking a little girl on his knee. Aunt Augusta had at last had to part with her cat basket, which was stuffed into the overcrowded luggage van.

'It's a crying shame!' she protested bitterly.

'What?' asked Werner.

Paolo grinned from the other side of the carriage.

Aunt Augusta did not answer. She pressed her colourless

lips together and stared in a hard and accusing manner at Mrs Rähmi's baby, which was yelling at the top of its voice while its mother carefully changed its nappy. She dropped the dirty one under the seat between someone's suitcase and someone else's basket.

The little train chugged slowly between the high white walls of snow along the side of the slope, with the high mountains towering on either side. Swiftly revolving blades whirled the falling snow away from the rails and flung it to the sides of the track. As the people nearest the windows stuck their heads out they saw gangs of workmen and sappers, who stood still on the railway embankment or flattened themselves against the snow walls and stared after the train with anxious faces.

Hundreds and hundreds of men had been at work on the line during the last few days, trying to get it clear, not only here but all over the Alps. They worked in shifts throughout the twenty-four hours, using the most modern snow-ploughs and track sweepers, but to keep the lines clear of snow when fresh avalanches and snowfalls were constantly coming down was impossible. During the last week 300 avalanches had fallen on the line over the St Gotthard pass alone.

'And clearing up the mess isn't a safe sort of job – not by a long chalk.' It was the old gentleman sitting in the corner who had spoken.

What he said was no news to anyone. He sat staring at each of the people in the carriage in turn, as though willing them to answer. The truth was that he was dreadfully anxious about his sons, one of whom had had to stay behind in Glarmatt while the other was working as a technical expert with the sappers. Their father wanted to talk, simply to forget his worries.

At last a pale little woman with two little girls, who had spent the night in the waiting room with the others, answered him. She held herself very straight under her black hat, with her arms held comfortingly round the toddler on her knee, and stared at him fixedly with large, anxious eyes.

'My husband's been called up,' she said. 'The whole battalion had to go and work at clearing the snow. As if their work isn't needed at home in Glarmatt! He's been sent to Urteli.' She sounded bitter.

'My youngest son's been sent to Prätigau,' the old gentleman began again. 'They've had three avalanches there but there's a threat of more. They're going to blast them down with explosive. My son is an expert.'

'Isn't that dangerous?' asked Jean Pierre eagerly under the reproachful gaze of the grown-ups.

'Dangerous?' said the old gentleman almost angrily. 'Of course it's dangerous. They think they know a lot these days, but they haven't enough experience. There haven't been such heavy snowfalls for half a century.'

'Rescue work is dangerous too,' said the woman, pulling down her little girl's skirt nearly over her knees. 'Near Afenberg a workman was buried while he was simply doing his job of clearing the road. A rescue squad set out with a dog and found him, but while they were busy giving him artificial respiration another avalanche came down and buried the whole lot of them.' She stopped, and then she said with a catch in her voice: 'And now they've called my husband up and sent him to help with the rescue work at Urteli!'

Werner had flushed scarlet while they were talking. He could hardly bear to listen. This woman's husband might actually be one of the soldiers who were still searching for his father and mother through the solid snow that filled the ruins of their home.

'Sometimes ten of the rescue squad risk their lives to dig out two bodies and when they've got them out they're dead,' said one of the soldiers moodily. He had a bandage round his head and looked ill; there were dark blue circles under his eyes and deep lines in his young brown face as if he had not slept for days.

'But if there's even a chance that they may be still alive –' spluttered young Finetti.

'Some chance!' answered the soldier.

'Even a ghost of a chance,' persisted Finetti fiercely. 'You *have* to go on so long as there's the smallest glimmer of hope. And don't *you* talk! I've watched you working during the last few days. And I saw your face when you dragged that little boy out alive from under the snow, just before the beam fell and gave you that biff on the head. You looked as if you'd been given a million dollars!'

The whole carriage was silent. The old gentleman heaved a deep sigh and nodded.

'Don't hang on to me like that, child!' said the anxious woman irritably, giving the smaller girl a little shake.

The little girl began to howl. Paolo sprang into action at once. He began to make faces, and when that was no good he began tugging at his right ear, letting out a different noise at each tug. By the time the old gentleman could bear it no longer, and burst out: 'Oh, do be quiet, boy!' Paolo had managed to coax an uncertain laugh out of the frail-looking little girl. But he was not yet satisfied with his success.

'Have you a tummy ache?' he demanded.

She shook her head energetically.

'Headache?'

She shook it again.

'Have you tickles between your toes?'

Shyly the little girl whispered, 'No.'

A violent jab in the back from Antti hinted that he should shut up. Paolo replied with a vigorous kick on Antti's shin and went on playing with the little girl.

'Why can't you laugh properly, then?' he asked her. 'Look! Like this,' and he produced a broad grin which her peaky little face could not hope to imitate.

Just at that moment he got a second jab from Antti and let out such a yell that Mr Hutamäki glared at him severely. This was all the unfortunate master could do at the moment, for he was helplessly penned in between the old gentleman in the corner and three of his own boys, who sat perched on each other's knees nearly burying him.

How Jean Pierre managed to jump down and wriggle to the window when they were all packed as tight as sardines remains a mystery, but he did, and pointed out of the window.

'Look! You don't see things like that where I come from.'

Everyone tried to peer out of the window and some of them succeeded. The train was running down a steep, narrow valley, and facing them, on the other side, a grey wall of rock towered up into the sky. Here and there a patch of snow was frozen fast to the sheer wall. A few wizened dwarf spruce firs which had somehow managed to take root in clefts and crannies, wore thick white wigs. Chasms between the rocks were filled with snow. Far below rushed the foaming torrent between banks covered with a fantastically shaped crust of snow and ice which had brought them suddenly close together, so that little was to be seen of the rock-strewn river bed.

'Just look at that!' exclaimed Jean Pierre, pointing to a zig-zag line of white on the other side.

It was the main road which descended from the pass in great hairpin bends, now completely snow-bound.

'There's the bridge!' cried Paolo, pointing down the valley. The bridge had become a huge white mound, straddling the river obliquely.

'I wonder how much of the bridge is left now,' said Hans Peter.

The train entered an avalanche gallery. On their left was the black wall of rock, on their right a series of reinforced concrete posts. The wide openings between them were nailed up with thick rough planks. Light filtered through narrow chinks.

They came out into the light again. The train chugged on down the valley. Now and then it passed gangs of workmen.

Now the valley broadened. Here, where the mountains rose less steeply, the blanket of snow was as thick as ever, with black streaks where the snow had slipped down clefts and gullies.

'In the St Gotthard district alone there are at least 500 known avalanche slopes,' said the old gentleman by the window. He had the best view, looking down the valley.

'Can you see Brachen yet?' asked Paolo hopefully.

'You young people are always so impatient,' answered the old gentleman rather scornfully.

'Pooh!' snorted Paolo. 'Me impatient! You should just see my granny! Compared with her I'm an old fogey! Why, she milks her goat in the mornings while she's still in her nightie and with only one foot out of bed, and during the day the sun's never hot enough for her 'cos she wants the curds to turn into cheese for supper the same night.'

The boys began to laugh. 'There he goes again!' grinned Holdert. 'I wish I could think up tales like that – I'd make a fortune when I'm grown up!'

'And suppose you did? What 'ud *you* do with a fortune?' demanded Paolo. 'I bet you *none* of you know what you'd do with a fortune if you had one!' he challenged them.

'Oh, don't we!' they jeered. 'Better than you, anyway!'

'Go on! I know exactly what you chaps want,' Paolo retorted. 'Cars and aeroplanes and trips round the world. And chucking all your money away on having a good time. Chicken and strawberries and cream every Sunday. That's not what I'd do at all. First I'd build a huge great orphanage with its own swimming bath and cinema. And I'd cram it full of the thinnest and dirtiest orphans I could find. And then I'd go to Brazil. I'd go myself and buy a big piece of land there, and then we'd fetch all the orphans out there. And when we'd earned enough money we'd build another orphanage and buy another piece of land. And we'd go on till we'd built a whole town in Brazil and there'd be no orphans left at home at all!'

The others shouted with laughter, even the grown-ups. Paolo faced them with flashing eyes. 'I *mean* what I say!' he cried. 'Werner's the only one who isn't laughing at me. My granny wouldn't laugh at me either. She'd say, "that's a good idea of yours, a very good idea, but you'd better leave out the swimming bath and the pictures".'

'Paolo,' said Mr Hutamäki gravely, 'you are a worthy descendant of a remarkable grandmother.'

'You don't know her, sir,' said Paolo. 'You've missed something!'

'We all know her from your stories – better than if we'd really met her and shaken hands with her,' Mr Hutamäki assured him.

'Do you mean that?' asked Paolo, beaming. 'D'you really mean that? I –'

He was interrupted by the shrill screech of the engine. The train ran into a tunnel. The lights came on abruptly, but they were only dim. Patches of black ice gleamed like rock crystal against the dark walls of the tunnel. Every now and then semicircular openings shot past. Huge icicles shone in every shade of blue and green against the granite walls. Here and there whole curtains of long thin icicles shimmered mysteriously. The daylight dazzled them when the train shot out of the tunnel again. Below them in the valley, a little above the river, ran the road.

'Look! The railing's gone!' cried Nikolai.

About twenty yards below the road the black railings lay snapped off, looking like a tiny toy in the snow. Only a small piece stuck up above the surface.

They ran into another avalanche gallery. This time it was made of reinforced concrete and sheet iron. There were openings here and there, giving glimpses of the valley down below.

But it was much nearer now and the mountains on the other side seemed to tower up higher than ever.

'We ought to be there fairly soon now,' said Mr Hutamäki.

The engine hooted again. They ran into another tunnel, rather shorter than the first but long enough. The snow-bright daylight hurt Werner's tired eyes as they ran out of it again.

'Oh, do look!' cried Paolo, pointing. 'The birds are practising formation flying!'

Sharply defined against the white slopes of the valley, a flight of ravens swooped in lovely curves. They wheeled and banked, first in large and then in smaller circles, cawing all the time. It was as if they were forming an escort for the train.

'They're hungry,' said Antti.

'Don't talk to me about being hungry, my tummy's rumbling already,' sighed Paolo.

'Would you like some strawberries and cream?' teased Antti.

'Or roast chicken?' asked François.

'Look there!' cried Paolo, pointing. He was very good at distracting the attention of the other boys. High above the white peaks flew an aircraft. It seemed to be losing height.

'I bet it's going to drop supplies!' said Paolo. 'I read about it in the paper.'

Proudly he hauled out of the pocket of his windcheater the old newspaper that he had been given yesterday. He had given it to Aunt Augusta to read, but after that he had stuck it in his pocket. 'It's the first time in my life I've ever had a newspaper of my very own,' he confided to her.

Now, with an important rustle, he unfolded the paper and opened it.

'The Federal Government of the Swiss Republic,' he began reading aloud solemnly, 'is proud to announce that its Air Force took prompt action to alleviate the distress in the remote villages which have been completely cut off and isolated by the phenomenal fall of snow. Never before in the history of the

Swiss Republic have help and self-sacrifice been so general and widespread, but never before has a natural catastrophe claimed so many victims.' Suddenly he began to stammer. He glanced timidly over the newspaper at Werner. Their eyes met. Paolo looked down quickly.

The engine hooted for the third time. The train was running more slowly now. They pushed into the darkness of the third and last tunnel. Conversation died.

Someone opened a paper parcel with much rustling and began to eat noisily. Everybody seemed to be listening to it. The walls of the tunnel slid past with their clusters of icicles and shining patches of ice. Aunt Augusta blew her nose. On the other side of the wooden partition a child that had been whimpering for some time broke into a howl. Its mother scolded it sharply.

'Just about seven minutes more and then we're there,' said young Finetti's voice hopefully.

Suddenly the brakes of the train screeched. Aunt Augusta's head bumped against the carriage wall behind her with such a jolt that her hat flew off. Paolo grabbed it. In the sudden, uneasy silence of the unexpected hold-up, no one but he noticed that the hitherto dauntless old lady was crying quietly. He bent forward quickly.

'Don't!' he whispered urgently. 'Don't! With grown-ups it only makes things worse.'

She stared at him in blank astonishment.

'Here. Your hat,' he went on, giving her his sweetest smile. He smoothed out a dent in the straw. 'Put it on. Nothing's happened really.'

The train had halted with a jerk in the dim light near the end of the tunnel. Everyone suddenly began to talk at once. Those who could stand on someone else's feet did so. Giuseppe and Paolo jabbered to each other in swift Italian. The Finns chattered to Mr Hutamäki in Finnish. Then there was silence as the door leading to the little platform at the end of the carriage opened and an icy draught blew in.

'Shut that door!' commanded the old gentleman.

A minute later a grey-haired ticket collector came in through the door in question. He pushed his way through the crowded central gangway, nodding to right and left in a friendly way as he passed. He made reassuring gestures with both hands and it was only when the buzz of talk had died down that he began to speak.

'We've got stuck in a small avalanche. Nothing serious has happened. But if any of the passengers would care to help clear away the snow – we've a railway engineer with us on the train and he can use all the help he can get.'

A quarter of an hour later a couple of dozen passengers, mostly men and boys, were crowded round the front of the engine. The little train had set out prepared for whatever might happen, and had brought enough tools to set a whole gang of helpers to work. The railway engineer who was travelling with them issued his instructions. Spades, picks, and snow shovels did good service and many people worked with their hands to clear away the stones, torn off branches, and masses of broken twigs that the snow had brought down with it. It was a landslide and had swept away everything that lay in its way for the whole length of its course, which ran down the mountain side in a fantastic cone of rubble. Only part of it had landed on the railway line, just in front of the mouth of the tunnel, and it was very lucky for everybody that the engine driver had jammed on his brakes at once.

The snow that had come down was black rather than white and smelled strongly of resin because of the freshly split pine wood. Very little was said. Even Paolo, who was working next to Werner, whispered when he had anything to say. White, feathery snow-flakes fell out of the grey sky and after an hour everything was pure white again: the slope down which the avalanche had rushed, the avalanche itself, the roof of the train and the shoulders of the men and boys working away in silence.

Once someone looked anxiously up the slope that the

avalanche had come hurtling down. Could anyone be sure that the same thing would not happen again? How long had they been working? It seemed like hours. Would they ever get to Brachen? The snow scoops on the engine could do nothing against this tightly packed snow. Every spadeful of it weighed pounds and pounds.

The railway engineer had got in touch with Brachen station by wireless. The electric snow-plough was on the way, and twenty men belonging to the railway were working away at the other side of the avalanche. The line might be cleared that afternoon.

At about twelve the snow stopped. A quarter of an hour later the sun broke through. The passengers, digging sturdily away, were much more cheerful. Werner, who was sweating like a horse, laughed at Paolo's jokes and at Jean Pierre tumbling about in the snow. In the half empty train young Finetti, who could be of no help in the work outside, went and sat down opposite Aunt Augusta. He had known her wool and apron shop all his life and now it had gone. He stared at her attentively, and when she looked up from Paolo's newspaper he said rather shyly:

'We've never seen so much of each other before.'

She looked hard at him through her glasses and said: 'You were one of the few boys who never teased me. You were always polite when your mother sent you with a message and you never made fun of my bandy legs. Does your arm hurt?'

Outside, the work of digging was getting on famously. They had made contact with the railway men at the other side of the avalanche and between them they had nearly dug their way through. High walls of dirty snow rose on either side of the railway line. The last bit of the obstacle was the worst. Whole tree trunks lay in the way. The snow-plough, which could do nothing against this kind of thing, had been sent back to Brachen. With axes, saws, and spades the last remains were cleared up.

'Another half-hour and we'll be through,' prophesied the grey-haired ticket collector, striding up and down the length of the train like a general encouraging his troops.

Then, before anyone expected it, the engine whistled again.

'They're through! We can go on!' cried Paolo.

But the young railway engineer standing on the step of the engine had other news for them. His face was drawn with anxiety as he shouted hoarsely: 'Into the train with you all at once! The engine's backing into the tunnel!'

Everyone leapt for the train. There was no time to ask why. But terror of the avalanche was clearly written on all their faces. Everything happened very quickly. The railway workers sprang on to the train as well and were carried into the tunnel. The little platforms at each end of the coaches were crammed full, the doors were not even closed.

There was a sudden thunderous roar followed by a deafening crash and the tinkle of falling glass. Everyone crouched down and clapped their hands over their ears. The blast blew through the tunnel like a hurricane. Paolo, with his mouth open, was flung over beside Werner, who pulled him up.

It was all over in a few seconds. One could feel a deep sigh of thankfulness go up from everyone. Thank God we were safely in the tunnel when it happened.

After a moment's deep hush an indescribable hubbub broke out, made up of every kind of human sound from crying and sobbing to hysterical laughter and happy shouts.

A few people had been cut by flying glass, but in their relief at finding themselves all in one piece no one thought much of a cut or so. Aunt Augusta's cheek had been cut by a splinter from the window and blood was trickling down, but she smiled bravely and young Finetti wiped the blood away.

A little later the elderly ticket collector walked through the carriages, a bloodstained handkerchief pressed to his cheek, to calm the passengers and explain what had happened.

The order to run the train back into the tunnel had come by

wireless and the railway engineer had picked it up and promptly carried it out. What had happened was that the great Bretschl avalanche had broken loose from the top of the Gluckner and come hurtling down. By far the greatest part of it would follow the usual route running over the Brachen avalanche gallery and would do no further harm, but an off-shoot of it would probably reach the railway.

This was exactly what had happened. The offshoot of the Bretschl avalanche had reached the railway line not far from the point where they stood, but far worse was the blast, whose terrific force could have flung the train down bodily into the depths.

'Oh well, we're more frightened than hurt, eh?' said the grey-haired ticket collector, giving Paolo a friendly pat on the shoulder. The boy had turned pale yellow and stared with quivering lips at the bloodstained handkerchief. The ticket collector laughed.

'Don't you worry about my handkerchief, young man. My old woman will stick it in the wash tub and that'll be that. But it was touch and go.'

He shook Jean Pierre's arm, nodded at Mr Hutamäki with an understanding look because he had so many boys to mother, and leaned over to speak to Aunt Augusta.

'You're in good hands with your son to look after you,' he said kindly with a glance at young Finetti, who smiled up at him because he did not think it worth while to explain the mistake. Werner felt ashamed and pushed through between François and Hans Peter to Aunt Augusta's side. But when he was there he could not do much for her, though Finetti made room for him.

The elderly ticket collector moved on, handing out cheery remarks like pills.

It was some time before it occurred to anyone to wonder what was going to happen to them now. Would they go on to Brachen? And how would they get there? Only one person actually asked. Most of the passengers could only think how lucky they were to be safe. And in the last few days and nights they had learned to be patient and to wait. The ordinary life that they had lived before the avalanche seemed almost unreal to them now – it all seemed so far away. They wondered if things would ever be the same again. Some of them had lost so much that they dared not think about it.

Hours went by. The electric bulbs burned more dimly. It began to get very cold.

'The juice is running out,' said someone.

None of the passengers were allowed to leave the train. Outside the tunnel dusk began to fall. The elderly ticket collector came round regularly to say a few cheery words and bring the latest news. A detachment of sappers had come out from Brachen to help the railwaymen to clear the new mass of rubble from the line. They would work through the night by the light of acetylene flares.

'I've seen a lot of things in the forty-three years I've worked on the railways,' he said, 'but the things that have happened in this last week I've never seen before in all my born days.'

Next time he came round Mr Hutamäki was trying in the dim and cheerless light to keep up the spirits of his boys, who by now were dog-tired and inclined to be rather cross.

'There are carriages and carriages,' observed the ticket collector. 'In some of them you hear crying kids and complaining women. In others you hear grumbling and grousing. And there are some where the people sit frightening each other with grisly tales. But you in here are always cheerful.'

Mr Hutamäki murmured some embarrassed reply. He was annoyed with himself for not succeeding better. But the boys were cold and hungry. Paolo was the only one who had been lucky enough to drop off to sleep. He lay like a little child with his head against Werner's shoulder.

All the food they had brought with them was eaten up, so

that they were hungry as well as cold. And it was hunger that made the Greek boy Nikolai say suddenly:

'I wish I had a sausage, a great thick, fat sausage, one of those juicy ones where you feel the juice spurting into your mouth.'

'Nikolai wants a sausage,' said Jean Pierre, 'but I should like a bowl of soup. A great big enormous bowl of soup with the fat floating about on it in circles as big as – as big as – well, awfully big, anyway.'

This was the beginning of the game. Aunt Augusta wanted her own bed, which was scattered in little bits down the mountain side, and the young soldier with the bandage round his head wanted a long-playing jazz record. Jussi had to think for so long that young Finetti spoke out of his turn.

'I just want a nice warm bite of something or other, I don't care what,' and then Jussi said: 'So do I.'

At this moment the ticket collector appeared again. He had brought the little red-haired English girl who had sat next to Werner the night before. She recognized him at once.

'Hullo,' she said softly.

'Hullo,' he answered shyly.

'I've brought her along because she's alone,' said the fatherly old ticket collector, 'and because you in here speak all sorts of languages.'

'Where is your father?' asked Werner in careful English.

'Oh, then you *do* speak English!' cried the little girl, surprised.

Werner tried to make room for her, with the result that Paolo woke up and Jean Pierre fell off Holdert's knees.

'You boys can sit on the floor,' Mr Hutamäki decided.

'My father's helping clear away the avalanche. He's able to because he's an officer in the sappers,' said the little girl with some pride.

'We're going to play a game,' announced Mr Hutamäki in English, which most of the boys understood. 'We'll take it in turns to say one after another what we want most. We've had sausage and soup. Hans Peter, it's your turn.'

'I want the next ski-ing holiday,' said Hans Peter firmly.

'I want Coco,' said Giuseppe. Coco was the donkey at the children's village.

'And I want summer and sunflowers. And a game of football on a warm evening when everything is green and there isn't a patch of snow *anywhere*,' said Nikolai.

'And you Greeks'll lose again, I bet!' Jean Pierre jeered at him.

Nikolai shrugged his shoulders. 'It's all one to me,' he murmured vaguely.

It was Werner's turn now. He said nothing. They looked at him expectantly but he still said nothing. His face slowly turned dark red and he shuffled his feet restlessly. 'I can't think of anything,' he said gruffly at last.

Paolo saw his Adam's apple going up and down. Werner sat and sobbed again and again. Suddenly Paolo could bear it no longer.

'You silly clots!' he burst out. 'You all know what Werner wants most. He's wishing his house was still standing and his father and mother still alive and all of them sitting round the table together – and him chopping wood for his mother and her scolding him because his shoes are worn through again – and his father telling him off for getting home late and then all of them laughing about it together next day!' His voice quivered. Mr Hutamäki stretched out a long arm and laid a hand on his sleeve to quiet him, but Paolo shook him off and went on excitedly: 'We've all longed for things like that. But it was a long time ago. I know I cried and cried and cried till I was all in and dropped off to sleep in my granny's arms, and as soon as I woke up and had had a meal I started all over again. I don't know what you fellows did, but we've all had the same thing to face. Our fathers and mothers were shot or died of disease or were missing or simply died of a broken heart. But we're all still alive, we laugh and play football and do our lessons and have all sorts of plans for the future. And – and – and we play games like this about what we want most, and one says a sausage and another says Coco and it's just fun for us. But Werner can't make a game out of it yet. It isn't fun for him. Can't you silly clots understand that? He's at the stage where he can only sob, and I wish I could give him a jolly good kick in the pants and make him howl, because that's much better. It makes things easier and you get through the worst bit quicker. He should yell at the top of his voice, but he doesn't. He just bottles it all up, the silly chump. He –' He stopped suddenly. He had worked himself up into quite a state and was hoarse with shouting. But now what he had wanted happened. Werner sat leaning forward with his elbows on his knees and his hands in front of his face. He was shaken with wild, hoarse sobs and his whole body trembled. Little Winifred, who looked rather frightened, laid a small brown hand timidly on his shoulder and glared indignantly at Paolo, whose ferocious speech she had not been able to understand, only to hear.

Paolo gave a long, quivering sigh, flopped down on the seat and said: 'That will do him good.'

In the long silence that followed, broken only by Werner's sobs and the sound of shuffling feet on the carriage floor, Winifred at last said softly and clearly in English:

'What *I* want most is my toy animals.'

Werner's sobs grew quieter. He blew his nose and wiped his eyes, but still kept his face hidden.

'Werner's father was the best man I have ever known,' said Aunt Augusta in a high and rather quavering voice. 'And Werner's mother was a good wife and mother. God rest their souls.' She blew her nose rather shakily. She was sitting too far away from Werner to be able to touch his hand and even if she could have she would not have done it. The Altschwanks had never been in the habit of showing their feelings.

It was very quiet in the carriage. One of the little girls whispered something to her mother, who shook her head. Everyone felt frightfully embarrassed and they were all wrestling with their own feelings. Such amazing things had happened in the last few days. What would it be next?

Young Finetti cleared his throat twice, but he could not bring himself to say what he wanted to: that Werner could always rely on his help and friendship whenever he needed it.

At last Mr Hutamäki spoke. Werner's shoulders were still shaking and no one could see his face in the dim light, but he was calmer now and may have understood what Mr Hutamäki said:

'Werner saved Paolo's life two days ago. And very possibly he and his father saved us all by coming and showing us the safe way down. Paolo will be his friend for life and so shall we all. He can always count on our help if ever he needs it. And it's probably a good thing that he's had a good cry with us all here; it wasn't natural that we should none of us say a word about his trouble. We shall all get on better together after this.' He paused and stuck out a large hand. 'Shan't we?'

It was a little time before Werner looked up; then he slowly put his hand into Mr Hutamäki's. There were still tears on his cheeks, but he was not ashamed of them any more. The beginning of a smile quivered round his mouth.

'Thank you, sir,' he mumbled softly. Then his eyes wandered to Paolo. They gave each other a long look. It was a look of understanding, such as old friends exchange. Paolo's great black eyes were serious and his voice softer than usual as he said:

'If I hadn't got all these Finns round me I'd give you a good hug, the way we do in the South. But they always laugh at me. The only thing these wretched northerners can do is to break all the bones in your hand.'

Some of the boys burst out laughing. The uncomfortable feeling had gone and they could start chattering again.

In the meantime the train had grown icy cold. The light from the electric bulbs had grown very dim indeed, and the walls of the tunnel reflected the harsh light from the acetylene flares which had been set up a little way off to light the work on the avalanche. 'How much longer are we going to be stuck here?' everyone wondered.

Presently the old ticket collector came along to bring them the answer. It had just been decided that the train should spend the night in the tunnel, but the passengers would be taken down to Brachen in groups. Ski patrols were on the way up to escort them down. A small number could spend the night in the carriage next to the engine, which could be warmed a little. In any case all the women and children were to be taken down to Brachen. Everyone was asked to get ready. Half an hour later the passengers were being led in long black lines by soldiers and a few station officials from Brachen along the rails through the deep cutting which the emergency squad had already made through the avalanche. The white walls towered many feet above their heads. Where the latest avalanche had come down it was difficult going. They had to clamber over tree trunks and branches, but the soldiers were there to help them. At one point a huge spruce lay prone, its roots sticking up vertically in ghostly outlines against the sky. But when once they got into the avalanche gallery the way was easier. Men with torches were stationed at intervals to light them on their way. Here at last the evacuees could see each other's faces. Werner, who had one of the pale little girls on his back, saw Bartel Gurtnelli helping Old John and his wife along, and went over to walk with them, though he had no free hand to help. A little in front were Mrs Rähmi, with her baby howling disconsolately, and the Reglis, lugging their hamper of chickens between them as they stumbled along. In the contrast of brilliant torchlight and deep shadow the familiar faces looked strange.

There was very little talk. Everyone was anxious and everyone was tired. Soldiers carried the stretchers with the injured. Winifred trotted along holding her father's hand. Paolo trailed along with Aunt Augusta; he was carrying the cat basket, and now and then a gentle, plaintive miaow rose up from it. Behind them in the distance they heard the mooing of the cows, left behind unmilked in the cold cattle trucks. They could not be helped till next morning.

In the large warm waiting room at Brachen the Red Cross had made preparations to receive the travellers. There were rows of camp beds. There were piles of blankets. There was a First Aid Post. There was hot food and coffee and warm milk for the babies. Willing hands helped to undress and comfort those who could not do it for themselves. There were even hot water bottles for the old people.

Old John's wife, lying snug in bed, murmured softly with her toothless mouth: 'And I've never had a hot water bottle before in all my life!'

10

NEWS ON THE WIRELESS

BRACHEN was crammed to overflowing. Travellers from the long-distance trains held up by the snowfall filled the hotels. Evacuees from the threatened mountain villages were billeted on private families. The large waiting rooms next to the station restaurant had been cleared to receive refugees. The proprietor of the restaurant, who normally did a thriving business, had handed over his kitchen and his coffee machines to the Red Cross and his staff were working as volunteers.

The wireless had been moved to the left luggage department, where it was kept turned on all day, so that anyone who wanted to could listen to the latest reports on what was happening in the threatened districts.

In the early morning light the long platform stretched away, lonely and deserted. No express trains stopped there now for a few bustling minutes before speeding away again. Everything looked grey: the rails, the dirty snow, the trucks in the siding and the long green Lucerne–Rome express, which had been standing for eight hours and thirty-two minutes, waiting for the signal to move.

A few railwaymen in blue overalls and black caps moved about. Now and then the sound of lowing came from one of the cattle trucks that stood in a siding under the broad station roof. The heads of three white oxen with great dewlaps gazed out mildly through an opening. The heavy snow-ploughs stood in another siding. Two soldiers in overalls were working on them.

At seven the wireless began to give the first news bulletins. A little group of evacuees and three of the station officials gathered in front of the left luggage office. People with pale, sleepy faces climbed down out of the waiting train and joined them.

The Pestalozzi boys straggled out of the warm, stuffy waiting room into the clear, frosty morning outside. Paolo, with his black curls standing on end, was yawning his head off. As soon as they saw the group on the platform and heard the familiar voice of the announcer, they came rushing along to listen. All except Werner, who trailed along behind them with his hands in his pockets and a reluctant expression on his face. He came and stood a little behind the group, half turned away, and listened too.

'During the last twenty-four hours,' said the announcer, 'another eight to twelve inches of snow have fallen on the northern slopes of the Alps, in the district south of the St Gotthard and in Goms. In places the temperature near ground level is in the neighbourhood of thirty-seven degrees Fahrenheit, a most unusual circumstance at this time of year, making the danger of fresh avalanches extremely great at the moment. The wind is veering to the south-east, thereby increasing the danger.

'Numbers of villages and valleys are completely cut off. Civil and military aircraft are working at high pressure to carry relief to the people in the isolated districts.

'The Co-operative Society of Davos has telephoned Zurich airport asking for fifty pounds of yeast to be sent for the bakeries. This has been dropped by aircraft over Davos so that the bakers there can make bread for the ten thousand inhabitants.

'The men working on the dam at Mauvoisin in the Valais are also being kept supplied by aircraft.

'Military aircraft are making regular reconnaissance flights over all valleys. Besides food they have dropped instructions as to the code to be used by the inhabitants to make known their needs.

'There is to be a big food drop in the Brachen valley, which has been completely cut off since yesterday by five great avalanches on road and railway. Through trains from Italy have been diverted and are now running through the Simplon Tunnel.

'At Santa Maria, in the Münster valley, the villagers wrote "oil" in enormous letters in the snow and marked the place for the drop with a Swiss flag. Forty gallons of diesel oil were dropped for use with the snow-plough.

'In the lower Engadine, machine parts had to be dropped, and a lathe for repairing a snow-plough.

'The G.P.O. has had to appeal to the Air Force for help in distributing the mails. This is being done by a Junkers 52 from the military airfield at Dübendorf. In view of the softness of the snow, mail bags are being dropped without parachutes, but medical supplies and packages marked "fragile" are being lowered by parachute.

'We are thankful to say that no new names have to be added to the long list of victims broadcast yesterday evening. Indeed, we are able to announce several extraordinary rescues of people and animals.

'In Zuoz a little boy called Peter Casty was down in the cellar when an avalanche smashed his home. He lay under a bench and kept calling for help, but none of the rescue squads heard him. Then he dropped off to sleep. Next morning he woke up and started calling again. This time someone heard him and he was dug out alive.

'At St Niklaus near Zermatt two girls rushed for shelter from the avalanche and hid in a cow-house a long way from the village. The roof collapsed on them and they were buried under masses of snow. But the postman had noticed them running there; he fetched the villagers and after hours of digging the two girls were pulled out unharmed.

'At Realp twenty-one sheep were rescued after being buried under the snow for 100 hours. The force of the avalanche pushed the hay down out of the loft into their stall, so that they were not even hungry.

'A most remarkable rescue is reported from Urteli. After fifty-seven hours of search and digging the rescue squad was able to extricate the village schoolmaster and his wife. Both are seriously but not dangerously injured and have been flown to Dübendorf. This rescue was successful thanks to the incredible endurance of the rescue squads and to a heavy roof beam which protected the victims from the force of the avalanche.'

The moment he heard the word 'Urteli', Werner began to sidle quietly nearer, hesitating now and then. He stood still on the fringe of the group between Antti and Hans Peter, gripping each by an arm. His face was working and he let out a few sounds that may have sounded like sobs but weren't. As the announcer ended, all the blood drained away out of Werner's face, he stood stock still, fighting back the happiness that sprang up within him. He could not believe it yet.

The group around him sprang into movement. Paolo, who had managed to wriggle into the front row, was suddenly by his side. He did not say a word. He did not even squeeze Werner's hand. He just stared at him.

'Come on,' said Werner abruptly.

The other boys followed them. They walked some way up the platform and stopped again, not knowing what to do. Suddenly Paolo began to jump up and down. Hans Peter and Antti wrung Werner's hand and muttered something unintelligible. Paolo rushed away to the waiting room where he found Mr Hutamäki, in shirt and trousers, trying to shave in front of a tiny mirror. Paolo grabbed his arm and shook it and told him the wonderful news in a hoarse whisper.

Mr Hutamäki wiped the soap off his face with the first thing that came to hand, which happened to be his sweater. With the arms of it tied round his neck and his face half shaved, he flung out of the waiting room and in three strides was at Werner's side.

The boy half fell against him. Mr Hutamäki steadied

him with one large hand and patted his shoulder with the other.

'We're so glad for you, Werner,' was all he could say.

*

From that moment Werner was a different boy. Different from what he had been before the accident. Bartel Gurtnelli, who had known him all his life and been to school with him, stared at him and could not believe his eyes. Werner chattered, Werner laughed. Werner, who had always been rather quiet and kept himself to himself, though he was well liked by the other boys in the village, dropped his reserve and started joking and fooling about.

It was as if he had suddenly been shaken awake.

When Bartel had congratulated him on the news he stood staring into the distance. This new Werner was a stranger, this Werner who had flung his arms round Aunt Augusta and given her a smacking kiss on both cheeks where the tears were still running down the wrinkles. And all the boys from the children's village seemed to be with him in the seventh heaven. Bartel smiled rather bitterly. He had been very early in the morning to the hospital where the sick and injured had been sent the night before, but he had not been allowed to see his parents. Now he felt twice as lonely as before.

At midday they were all given a hot meal and Werner ate like a wolf. After that Mr Hutamäki took the boys into Brachen. Bartel walked part of the way with them. The sun was shining, even the wind seemed warm, and their boots sank into the soft, wet snow in the streets. Though this was a bigger village than Glarmatt, with more traffic, the snowed-up houses looked the same here as everywhere else. Two men were standing on a high, snow-laden roof, sawing the frozen snow into square blocks. The high, square belfry had on a funny white cap and looked a dirty pink colour against the white background of mountains. The streets were steep and narrow and there were a lot of stone houses colour-washed a dirty yellow or yellowish pink.

At a street corner Bartel raised a hand. 'I turn off here. Be seeing you.'

'Where's he going?' asked Werner.

'To the hospital where his father and mother are,' answered Hans Peter.

Werner said nothing. He stood staring after Bartel. Slowly he began to realize that perhaps he ought to be anxious about his parents. They were lying injured in some hospital or other. Perhaps they were in pain; perhaps they were suffering from shock like Bartel's father and mother. But in any case, each of them knew that the other was safe and that he was safe too. No, Werner shook his head. No, he simply could not be anxious any more. For him anxiety was a thing of the past.

Two aircraft circled above the village. They came lower and lower.

'I bet they're going to drop things!' cried Paolo. 'Can't we go and look at the dropping zone?'

Of course they got there too late. The containers fell while the boys were still among the last of the houses. When they got nearer, they saw that the whole of the dropping zone was cordoned off with troops, so that they could not have got there anyway. They had to stand and watch from a distance. The dropping zone was a wide shallow hollow marked out with flags laid on the ground. The containers lay scattered all over the hollow. Long yellow streamers were fastened to them to make them easier to find. Some of them lay buried deep in the snow. Men were gathering them up and loading them on to sledges to bring down to Brachen.

All the way there and back Werner smiled at everyone they met. He even said 'Hullo!' to people he did not know, and he looked down with a feeling of inward pleasure on this village that was so much larger and more important than his own.

'But wooden houses are better,' he decided. 'This plaster stuff peels off. Urteli is prettier.'

'You should come up to *our* village,' said Paolo. 'Spick and span houses. Built them ourselves. Fresh as a new pin. The most beautiful houses in the whole of Switzerland.'

'I'll come and see them some day,' promised Werner.

There were more strangers walking about the village: stranded train passengers in town clothes, ladies in mink, gentlemen in fur-lined overcoats. There were a great many soldiers and volunteers. The people who looked least at home were the peasants evacuated from the neighbouring villages. Some of them stared eagerly, absorbing all the new sights, others had a dazed look in their haggard eyes and did not speak at all.

In the waiting room Old John and his wife were still in their camp beds. They had just been brought a cup of coffee and were enjoying it audibly, sitting up in bed side by side. Their cane travelling basket and two small black bundles lay on the floor at the foot of the beds.

'We've never been so pampered in our lives before,' said Old John, giving Werner a broad, toothless grin as he came in. 'Here's health to you, young man, and to your father and mother. They'll have as little to complain about in the way they're looked after as we have.' He raised his cup of coffee, nodded to Werner with a wink, and went on sipping his coffee with obvious pleasure.

When he had finished, he put his empty cup on the floor beside his wife's.

'Now you just watch, young man. These will be cleared away in no time. We're being waited on like the President of Switzerland and his wife. Look, here she comes.'

A pretty girl wearing a white armlet came over to fetch the empty cups which stood on the floor between the camp beds. She nodded to Werner, who stooped down and put the cups on her tray, smiling into her face.

'Aren't you the boy who . . .?' she asked.

'Yes, that's me.'

'Splendid,' she said. 'It isn't many who have so much luck.'

'And now me and my old girl are going to stretch out again and have a good lie in,' announced Old John, settling down on his side. He glanced up at the ceiling. 'It's only a pity I'm not a bit deaf. That baby of Mrs Rähmi's yells its head off here just the same as it did at home.'

It was perfectly true. A baby's piercing howls came from the floor above. The station master's wife, who had a flat above the station restaurant, had been very kind and had taken in not only Aunt Augusta's three cats but the sick Rähmi baby as well.

'When it isn't howling, it's quite a nice child,' added Old John, running his hand over his stubbly chin with a rasping noise. 'There he goes again!' And winking at Werner he snuggled down in bed.

His wife was lying quite still in bed with her eyes shut. She seemed utterly tired out. On her other side Aunt Augusta sat up in bed with five hairpins between her pursed lips. She plaited her thin iron-grey hair into two wiry little pig-tails and fastened them into a bun. When she had taken all the hairpins out of her mouth, she looked up at Werner and snapped: 'You needn't stand there staring!'

He laughed and gave her an orange that he had bought.

'They're sour, those things, but people say they're healthy,' said Aunt Augusta tartly, but she turned pink with pleasure. It was easy to see that she was pleased with the gift.

After dark that evening, just before supper, nine new evacuees were brought in. They came from Valgretto, a tiny hamlet in a little valley high up above Brachen. One of them was a boy of about eleven, who was sobbing. Two women in black coats and with black shawls over their heads tried in vain to comfort him. They looked as if they had been crying too, and there were black smears on their faces as if they had wiped the tears away a good many times with dirty hands. An old couple and one or two silent men with grim faces followed them.

They came and sat in the corner farthest from the door, near to the shining coffee-machines, and were at once served with everything. They were given large plates of hot sausages and potatoes and great mugs of hot coffee. But it was as if they did not realize what was going on, they just stared sombrely before them. They hardly even glanced at each other. The boy just went on sobbing. He wouldn't eat anything, and when one of the women poured the warm coffee down his throat he brought it all up again. The other woman wanted to take off his sweater and trousers and put him to bed, but he began screaming and fought her off. He was determined to keep all his clothes on. Finally he was tucked into bed, clothes and all. They took off his boots, but he kept on everything else. He lay on his tummy with his face in his hands and went on crying. Now and then he flung up his head and shouted something and kicked with his feet under the blankets. The grown-ups with him shook their heads as much as to say, 'No no, this won't do.' The other people in the room could not understand what he said.

Everyone in the waiting room, who had cheered up after the good news from Urteli, felt depressed and miserable again. There was no more laughter and people whispered instead of talking out loud.

Paolo, who was burning to go and find out what it was all about, went and offered to help with the coffee-machines. When he was told they did not need him, he still hung about. He found a corner where he could squat down. Now he was not far from the boy, who was still sobbing. When no one was looking, he crept nearer. Other evacuees came over to the group of newcomers, eager to hear what it was all about and what had happened at Valgretto.

It appeared that this morning three avalanches had come hurtling down the mountains, one after the other, with a noise like thunder. When the last dull thud had echoed away down the valley, cries for help came from a small group of houses lying rather close together. Neighbours hurried to the spot and began rescue operations at once. One of them started off on skis to fetch help.

All that was left of three houses, a sawmill and five cow-houses was some smashed weather-boarding, broken beams, torn-off windows, doors and gutters, pots and pans and bales of hay scattered over the snow. After several hours' work, nine people were dug out alive and one old man who was dead. Thirty-eight cows were smothered under the snow. Three people were still missing: the father and mother of this boy and his little sister.

The boy himself was standing on the roof of his home, clearing away the snow, when the avalanche struck it. He was flung far away but was quite unhurt.

A rescue squad had come up from the valley to help in the search for those missing, but none of them had been found yet. The boy had been in a dreadful state of mind, and had refused to leave the place when the officer commanding the rescue squad gave orders to stop the search because of the danger of further avalanches. Everyone had now left Valgretto. The boy, Klaus Watzig, had refused to budge and they had had to pick him up and carry him away. He would not listen to reason. He had just gone on crying out that his father and mother had been in the cow-house and his little sister in the shed and that they simply must be there still. But there was no sign of the shed, it had gone. And the cow-house lay in ruins.

More and more evacuees gathered round the little group from Valgretto. These people who had been so silent at first now grew more talkative. Again and again they told each other the story of all they had been through.

Klaus raised his head now and then to listen. His face was swollen and wet with tears; he glanced round instinctively in search of other young faces, and he found Paolo, Nikolai, and

Werner close to him. Bit by bit they wormed their way nearer as the grown-ups formed a separate group. In the end Paolo was sitting on Klaus's bed.

No one said much, not even Paolo. Klaus repeated for the hundredth time that his mother and father had been in the cow-house and his little sister in the shed and that they must still be there. His voice was weak and trembling, with now and then a long, high sob.

'They're *still there*,' he repeated obstinately. 'And now the search has been stopped till tomorrow morning because the snow will freeze hard tonight and in the morning the sun will be off that side of the valley. I heard them say so myself.'

Werner remembered the report on the wireless that morning: 'Thanks to the incredible endurance of the rescue team . . .' At home at Urteli they had searched all night long by torchlight. But the danger of fresh avalanches varied from place to place. All the same, it was dreadful to think of those people left behind while there was still a chance that they were alive. 'Even the ghost of a chance,' young Finetti had said, 'you have to go on so long as there's the smallest glimmer of hope.' It was a pity he was at the hospital now.

Klaus's tear-stained, freckled face under his unruly mop of hair looked woe-begone against the blue and white check pillow-slip on the camp bed. The eyes beneath the red, swollen lids were imploring help. But who could help him?

By now it was late. The lights were dimmed to half strength. Mr Hutamäki collected his boys and drove them to bed. But Werner stayed with Klaus a minute or two longer. He squatted down beside him and said:

'My father and mother were buried under the snow for fifty-six hours and they were got out safely last night.'

Klaus said nothing at first, then he mumbled something that Werner could not catch.

'What did you say?' asked Werner, bending closer.

'I said how splendid for you,' whispered Klaus.

'I mean,' said Werner, 'that your parents may be all right, too.'

Klaus shook his head slowly. 'Mother isn't strong,' he said, 'and my sister's quite little.'

'You never know,' said Werner. 'Once they got a man out alive who'd been buried eighty hours under the snow.'

Klaus nodded, but he looked as if he did not believe it.

'It's true,' said Werner. 'And today I heard of a man who'd been buried four and a half days. He was just going to start off to California and had his passage paid and everything. But he went up for the last time to milk his father's cows, up in the cow-shed. And then the avalanche came. But he got hold of a great wooden beam and worked his way up it like a bear climbing up a pole. When they found him at last unconscious he'd worked his way sixteen feet up. Just before they found him he'd been dreaming he was in California already and earning good wages.'

'And is he still alive?' asked Klaus, round-eyed.

'Well, it happened more than sixty years ago,' Werner admitted, turning rather pink, 'but I only heard about it today. From a lady in a shop. He was her uncle. But it shows it *can* happen.'

Klaus gave him one look and then turned his back to him.

'Is there anything you'd like before I go to the others?' Werner asked. The big room had grown very quiet. Everyone had settled down to sleep.

Klaus's only answer was to pull the bedclothes over his head.

Werner went back to his own bed. It was between Antti and Paolo; they were both wide awake still, of course. He took off his outer clothes and crept into bed. Lying on his back with his hands clasped behind his head, he stared at the ceiling. Except for the snores of the sleepers and the whispers of those who were still awake and the creak of the door when anyone went in or out, the big room was quiet. But try as he would he could not go to sleep.

11

THE RESCUE

IT seemed to Werner that he lay awake for hours. After some time he heard a gentle and regular buzzing that sounded above and through the little noises made by the sleeping people. It was the central heating. Footsteps sounded in the flat above. Mrs Rähmi's baby began to cry again. Someone sighed gustily. There seemed to be more sounds as the night wore on. Beside him Paolo tossed and turned on his bed, nearly throwing off the blankets. The moon shone through the uncurtained upper part of the windows.

In a pause in the noises Werner heard the sound of sobbing. That must be Klaus crying again. The sobs sounded smothered, as if he still had his head under the bedclothes. Werner felt more restless than ever.

Suddenly Paolo's face was close to his. 'Can't we *do* something?' he whispered.

'What can we do?' Werner whispered back. 'We can't go and dig them out ourselves.'

'Why not, if he shows us the way there? There are heaps of shovels and sounding rods in a shed in one of the sidings. I saw them myself.'

'Mr Hutamäki would never let you go,' said Werner.

'Of course not. But when he's asleep we can wake all the others and go along, the whole lot of us. It's not even dark outside. There's a moon.'

Werner began to feel very excited. There was absolutely nothing that he would rather do than this. He felt that if he had to stay in bed in this waiting room he would choke. He was burning to *do* something: dig, search, sound, to go on and on until they found those people who were having that terrible time under the snow like his parents, like himself not so long ago. Supposing they could find Klaus's parents and his little sister and dig them out alive. . . . Think if they died during the night because no one went on looking for them. . . .

Klaus was all to pieces as he himself had been for three days, except that he hoped his people were alive. Suppose *he* had still been hoping and the rescue team had stopped searching for *his* parents? What would he have done? He would have been quite desperate. He would have gone on searching all by himself till he found them. But Klaus was only eleven. They had picked him up and carried him away and he could do nothing but kick and scream.

Paolo was busily whispering to Antti. Antti sat up and nodded. Werner nudged Paolo.

'How shall we know when Hutamäki's asleep?' he whispered in a voice hoarse with excitement.

'I know a way,' said Paolo firmly. 'You just wait.'

After a little Werner heard a soft groan. It was Paolo. 'My tummy! Oh, I've got such a pain!' Werner heard him moan softly. 'Oh, I've got the most frightful tummy ache . . . it's dreadful . . . I can't bear it!' His voice rose painfully.

'Ssh!' called someone from the other end of the room.

A woman's voice whispered: 'Can I do anything for you?'

And Aunt Augusta's harsh voice was clearly recognizable as she told him, 'Go to the lavatory, child!'

'Oh, no!' moaned Paolo rather more softly. 'It isn't that. O – o – oh.'

A Red Cross nurse came out of the little room behind the big serving counter. She tiptoed carefully between the rows of beds. The boys were horrified. Of course. They might have known someone would be on duty!

'Oh, thank you, Nurse, it's better now, really much better,' whispered Paolo. 'Oh, don't bother, please. I've had this kind of pain in my tummy before. It doesn't mean anything.'

Werner felt ashamed as the nurse tiptoed away again. She

was not young and must be tired herself. But there was no sound from Mr Hutamäki. He must be fast asleep. That was certain.

Paolo leaned across to Werner and whispered in his ear: 'We'll go to the lav. one by one and not come back. I'll tell the others. You fetch Klaus.'

Antti had started off already. Paolo crept carefully along the row of beds where the other boys were sleeping. He waked them all except Hans Peter. Hans Peter was Mr Hutamäki's assistant. They couldn't possibly let him in on this.

Werner waited a few minutes that seemed like eternity. One by one he saw the boys slip through the door like ghosts. At last, with his clothes under his arm, he glided cautiously over to Klaus. The exhausted refugees around them slept deeply. No one stirred.

Klaus was lying still, but he jumped when Werner touched his shoulder. He turned over and Werner's hand brushed a very wet pillow. Klaus gave a gulp and a sniff and then asked:

'What's up?'

'Sh!' whispered Werner putting his finger on his lips. 'Come along. You're to show us the way up to your house, then we'll go on with the search. We know where to find the tools and there are eleven of us, counting you.'

Klaus shot upright in bed, panting with excitement. Without a word he slid out of bed, snatched up his boots and tiptoed to the door. Werner grabbed a jacket off the end of someone's bed. Its owner lay on his back snoring loudly. It was a good thing so many of them were snoring or tossing and turning. The noises that the boys made hardly sounded at all.

'Here!' he said when he got outside. It was icy cold. The wind was on this side of the mountains. Werner handed Klaus the windcheater which was far too large for him, and Klaus put it on. He looked ridiculous in it.

The others were waiting for them where they had arranged:

behind the shed at the end of the platform. Three blue lamps burned under the station roof, and these and the reflected shimmer from the snow gave a cold and ghostly light. A couple of small red lanterns between the rails were the only encouraging sight. Everything was perfectly quiet.

Armed with shovels and sounding rods the boys set out, with Klaus leading the way. They kept up a good pace. The snow, which had frozen over since nightfall, crunched under their feet. The village lay silent and unreal under its thick white blanket of snow. Lights showed in windows here and there in houses and in the hospital.

'We ought to have brought Bartel with us,' thought Werner, but now they were fairly on the way it was too risky to go back and fetch him.

'How long will it take us to get up there?' asked Antti. No one had thought of that.

'Three hours if we get a move on,' answered Klaus. He hardly seemed to be the same boy who had lain sobbing in the waiting room. Holdert had given him his own windcheater and put on the big one instead. Klaus was much more comfortable.

He set off at a brisk pace. They climbed quickly. Soon the village lay below them. Jussi glanced over his shoulder.

'It's just like a dream!' he whispered. Nikolai, walking beside him, shivered.

By the time they got there the moon stood high in the sky. Antti put the time at two in the morning. Around and above them the mountains towered motionless. The deeply trodden path by which they had come looked like a black ribbon in the snow. Some way away they could see a few houses and higher up, almost out of sight, some cowsheds.

'It's here,' said Klaus.

'Where?' they all asked at once.

There was no sign of a house. A few broken pieces of wood lay about, there were holes in the snow, a heap of beams and rubbish, an ugly black blot in this white, moonlit expanse.

'Where?' they asked again.

'Here!' cried Klaus impatiently. 'The cow-house stood here and the shed was there.'

'How can you know for sure?' demanded François. 'Everything's under the snow now. It must all be different.'

'It's here!' Klaus insisted with a quiver in his voice. 'The others wouldn't believe me, either. They would go and hunt over there – and there!' He pointed above the places where most of the wreckage lay. A piece of the snow-field had been marked off with little flags: the area that had been sounded by the first rescue party. But Klaus was standing a little farther to the left.

'It's here! here! here!' He stamped angrily in his own deep footprints. Then he struggled painfully round in a circle, sinking more than knee deep in the soft snow, breaking the frozen crust with a high, brittle sound.

'We ought to have brought a dog,' whispered Werner.

'How do we begin?' asked Paolo and looked at Werner. In the moonlight all their faces seemed to have lost all their colour.

'First search the area, then sound,' Werner decided, 'to see if we strike something. If we find anything, we'll dig.'

The sounding rods they had brought with them were heavy, old-fashioned things and the work was far more difficult than they had expected. In Urteli and later in Glarmatt they had seen the soldiers doing it: standing in a row at a short distance from each other, striking straight downwards with their rods, first beside the left foot, then between their feet, then beside the right foot. Then one step forward and begin all over again.

It was hard to stick the sounding rod straight down in the snow without slanting to either side. It was hard to haul it straight up again. Paolo could not manage it at all, he was too small. His whole face was contorted with the effort and he nearly wept with rage.

'Ready?' called Werner. 'Another step forward.'

But it was hard work. And who could say how many feet deep the snow was that they had to pierce? Who could be sure that Klaus had shown them exactly the right place? The country was strange to them and they could hardly believe that an avalanche had passed there at all. The snow was perfectly clean; there was no earth or rubble; no trees had been swept down. And there was no trace of the path of the avalanche.

The boys felt the bitter cold in their faces but soon they were dripping with sweat, most of them were panting with excitement and they worked at far too quick a pace. Slowly their hands grew numb with cold as they held the sounding rods. In their excitement some of them had forgotten to bring their mitts.

'We're an inexperienced crew,' Antti whispered to Werner.

Werner nodded. He was working the hardest of all. He had got the knack of handling the sounding rod now. But it was a slow job, exasperatingly slow. And he had to keep an eye on the others; they kept on jerking their sounding rods clumsily.

'Look out!' he warned them. 'If your sounding rod gets bent it'll leave gaps and we'll never find anything.'

Klaus was working by himself outside Werner's organized squad. He hadn't a sounding rod, but he had a wooden stick which was much lighter, though it was shorter. Sometimes he walked round snuffing like a dog, sounding with his stick now here, now there. He worked in a circle round the outside of the others but without much system. He was too restless for that and too anxious to get some result. He drove himself relentlessly, without a second's rest, and his eyes looked wild and feverish in the strange light of the moon.

The boys pricked row after row of little dark holes in the snow, only to trample on them when they took the next step forward. They felt as if they were sounding a huge area, but when Werner turned now and then and had a look round him he felt rather hopeless. They had sounded such a very small piece, and how long had they been at work?

The moon was low above the mountains now. In a few hours the sun would rise. It seemed to get colder and colder. Their bodies were damp with sweat and if they stood still for a moment their cold, clammy clothes stuck to them at once. Werner felt a long shiver run down his back.

They were working rather more than 150 feet above the valley with their backs to the slope. They were so engrossed in their work that most of them had forgotten the danger of a second avalanche on the same spot, though it was this danger which had forced the rescue party to give up yesterday. But it had been thawing then and the late afternoon sun had been shining on this south-westerly slope. The temperature had been below freezing point for several hours now and the danger must be very much less. Werner drove himself and the others without mercy and allowed them no rest, even when most of them were so tired that they felt ready to drop.

'Here!' shouted Jussi suddenly from the end of the row. 'I've found something. There must be something here!' The rod trembled in his hand as he pulled it out of the snow. Paolo and Holdert began jabbing wildly with their rods close to the same place.

'Here! Stop that!' cried Werner. 'We've got to do this carefully.'

With great care they formed a new line on either side of Jussi, who would not give up his place. Quivering with suspense they began poking through the snow again. Klaus, wild with excitement, cried:

'It's the cow-house! It must be the cow-house! Get a move on now, do!'

Just then Holdert and Antti struck something. A minute or two later Werner did the same. It looked as though Klaus were right. He had brought them to the right place.

'Let's start digging,' said Werner.

They were all glad to exchange the cumbrous sounding rods for snow shovels. But there were only eight shovels, so the boys who had none began grubbing with their hands. Klaus dug himself in like a rabbit till he was right down in a hole, but he got nowhere. What they had struck was a dozen feet below the surface of the snow.

'It may be a tree,' said Werner.

'There *wasn't* a tree!' shrilled Klaus frantically.

'Or tools, or a wood pile, or –'

'That was all in the shed and the cow-house,' cried Klaus.

'Or some of the wreckage that was carried away,' said Antti. He did not want Klaus to build on false hopes.

'But we're higher up than that,' Werner pointed out. He looked round at the untidy mass of smashed wreckage lying on the snow and at the trampled patches of snow where the rescue party had been searching and digging.

The boys dug and dug, each in his own way. No one gave up, but some of them were too tired to see what they were doing any longer. They went on digging aimlessly and with a kind of mist before their eyes. Neither Werner nor Antti was in a state to make them follow a definite system in their digging. Klaus dug a hole first here and then there. In the end they did not even know if they were still working above the spot where they had struck something with the sounding rods.

By now the sun was almost up. There was a warm rosy glow in the east, with grey misty clouds hanging before it like a thin curtain above the mountain tops. In the west the mountains were rose coloured, and those in the east had almost purple edges. But none of the boys had eyes for that. The hard, hopeless work through the long hours of the night had been too much for them. But they could not stop. Nearly crying from sheer tiredness they struggled obstinately on. Klaus kept fuming: 'They're here – they're here, I tell you!'

Suddenly they heard the thunderous roar which they were

getting to know so well. It was impossible for them to turn paler than they were already, but Paolo clapped his hands over his ears.

'I won't hear it!' he screamed through the full, booming noise.

The others stood still with anxious faces. Only Werner appeared unmoved. He listened carefully.

'I don't know where it is,' he said loudly, 'but it isn't here.'

He was right. A few minutes later everything was quiet again in the valley – deathly quiet. Where had it been? On the other side of the valley? Or further away on the same side as themselves? The sound had echoed round and round until they did not know where it came from. It seemed to come from all sides at once.

'We'll go on digging,' said Werner. 'Get cracking. We must go on so long as there's a ghost of a chance.' He said it mechanically as though he had to keep reminding himself of it.

They began to dig again in silence. Klaus had dug such a deep hole that there was nothing to be seen of him at all. The others were digging two deep trenches diagonally across the area that they had sounded. They were shoulder deep now. Werner knew that the snow they dug out ought to be cleared away, but they had no sledges. On each side of the trenches a high wall of snow was mounting up which increased the weight of snow over the part where they were digging.

'Werner, we can't go on like this,' whispered Antti who was working next to him.

Werner straightened himself up and ran his hand over his forehead. He saw stars, but blinking did not make things any better.

'Listen!' said Jussi suddenly.

There it was again. The grim, menacing roar of masses of snow hurtling down. Where was it this time? They strained their eyes but could see nothing. The terrifying echoes sounded all round them. But suddenly Nikolai pointed.

'There! Over there!'

Nearly opposite them on the farther side of the valley an avalanche was rushing down the slope, a narrow stream of great heavy lumps that sent a booming noise along the whole length of the valley. The whole thing lasted barely a minute, but in that one minute the avalanche must have travelled several thousand feet. It left a dirty stripe behind it in the snow.

While the boys stood watching, they heard a distant zooming. Shading their eyes with their hands they searched the sky. The sun had risen above the mountains now, but it was still low and the level light shone straight into their eyes. The zooming in the east grew louder, it grew to a roar, then to a loud roar and a moment later two aircraft flew low over the valley, swooping right over the heads of the boys.

Paolo began to shout and wave. He clambered up a wall of snow on hands and knees so as to get nearer to them, and stood still waving after them in disappointment as they flew on.

But they were banking and turning. They came back, flying lower still. The other boys began to wave and shout wildly as well. Werner and Antti held their snow shovels aloft, swinging them to and fro. Only Klaus stood watching in silence, glum and unhappy.

As the aircraft flew over for the third time, they dropped something out. Three parcels drifted down, hanging from little parachutes. Yelling with excitement the boys rushed forward, waving their arms and trampling through the deep snow to the places where the three parcels had landed. Long yellow ribbons trailed from them to make them easier to find. But only one parcel, the heaviest, plunged so deep into the snow that any searching was needed.

'We'll take them all to Werner!' yelled Paolo, who was staggering along with this last package and refused to give it up to anyone else for love or money. His voice sounded shrilly in the quiet peace of the valley, where silence had once more fallen. Only the echo repeated '—erner, —erner!'

Jussi and Giuseppe came struggling along from the left with the second package, and Nikolai, Holdert, and Martin with the third, all of them sinking thigh-deep in the snow like Paolo and François.

Opening the parcels was unexpectedly difficult. They were done up in heavy grey sacks and fastened round with thick, stiff wire, but Antti's clasp knife did wonders.

'Bread!' shrieked François. '*Du pain, du pain!*' He caught the other French boy, Jean Pierre, by the shoulders and began to dance round and round. But suddenly he caught sight of Klaus. He stopped at once, his arms fell to his sides and he stammered awkwardly: 'It's because I'm so frightfully hungry.'

All eleven of them stared down in silence at the ten large brown shiny loaves. No one touched them till Antti began cutting off huge hunks and handing them round. Klaus accepted one but hardly allowed himself time to eat it. Without glancing at the others he bit off a couple of large mouthfuls which he found it hard to swallow. He was not crying any more, he just stared straight before him.

Antti and Werner opened the second parcel between them. It was a First Aid outfit. There were medicines, packages of cotton-wool, some iodine, and a couple of tubes of pain-killing drugs. They did not know what to do with all this and packed it up again as best they could.

The third and heaviest parcel was full of provisions: a bag of sugar, a tin of coffee, six tins of bully beef, six tins of baked beans in tomato sauce.

'Oh, tomato sauce!' cried Paolo joyfully. 'Antti, where's your knife? It's got a tin-opener. We'll be able to dig lots better when we've had a good meal, you'll see! Give me beans in tomato sauce with garlic and I'll work like an ant moving house!'

'How are you going to warm up these beans of yours?' grumbled Martin with a contemptuous glance at Paolo, whose excitable manner got on his nerves more than it did with the other boys.

'Where *is* my knife?' asked Antti. 'I haven't got it. Didn't you have it, Paolo?'

'Where's Antti's knife gone?' they all asked at once.

'I put it down there in front of you,' declared Paolo, pointing to one of the sacks that had been used as wrappings.

They all began hunting for the knife, but without result.

'It must have fallen in the snow!' wailed Paolo. 'Oh, Antti, and it was such a lovely knife. It was a simply wizard knife. I'll give you a new one when I've saved up enough money.'

'That won't help us now,' grumbled Martin.

They hunted for it in the snow, but it had been trampled by so many feet since then that the task was hopeless.

'There's no point in going on digging any longer,' Werner decided half aloud.

Klaus, who had been standing with a stunned look on his face, raised his head sharply. Werner glanced at him and received a look which stabbed like a knife.

'I didn't mean that, Klaus,' he said at once. 'Of course we'll go on.'

Klaus tried to say something but his voice was drowned in the threatening roar, partly dulled by distance, of another avalanche.

'That was much farther away,' said Antti.

But the words were hardly out of his mouth when there was a thunderous crash followed by the familiar booming noise, but this time it was so near that they ducked their heads and clapped their hands over their ears or faces.

'Go away! Go away!' shrieked Paolo. 'Don't come here!' He seemed to pit his small person against the monstrous forces of nature. His voice sounded shrilly above the loud, reverberating crashes that followed swiftly one after another.

The boys felt as if some gigantic hand picked them up and threw them. They fell hither and thither, stumbling and screaming, and then were suddenly quiet again, for it was all over. They choked and coughed and spat snow out of their mouths. Jean Pierre and Martin had faces all red from scrapes and grazes and Holdert was holding his arm tight, his face distorted with pain.

'That was a near shave,' stammered Paolo as he gasped for breath. 'Now the worst is over, so sure as my granny was praying for us just now.'

François, who was still on his knees, pointed. 'Look at that!'

Less than fifty yards away the landscape had changed. The avalanche had altered the shape of the valley. Powdery snow was still rising in clouds. A tree had been swept down and was lying there just under the surface with its branches sticking up through the snow. But everything was still and quiet again.

'I think I've broken my arm,' said Holdert.

'I won't go on with this any more,' cried Jussi suddenly in a high, unnatural voice. 'I'm going back to Brachen. There's no point in all this digging.' He had taken a bad toss when the blast hit him and was all to pieces.

'Let me see your arm,' said Werner, going over to Holdert, who stumbled a couple of steps to meet him. Werner looked at the arm but he hardly dared to touch it. Forearm and upper arm made an odd-looking angle.

'It might be sprained,' he said doubtfully, 'or dislocated.'

Holdert clenched his teeth. 'I'm going back to Brachen with one of the others to see a doctor. I don't mind going with Jussi, even though he is squealing like a pig.'

Werner said nothing. The others stood staring at him. Without realizing it, they had come to look on him as their leader. Klaus, who was still coughing, glanced from one to another with a look of despair on his face. Were they going to give up? Had all this work been for nothing? Would he have to go away and leave them buried there *again*, his mother and father and Marie?'

'I won't go!' he shouted hoarsely between fits of coughing. 'I'm simply not going to leave this place. I won't!'

'I'm not going either,' said Werner. 'Who else will stay?' But his voice sounded discouraged and he looked round the ring of sombre, staring faces without much hope.

'I'll stay,' said Antti.

'I'm going back with Holdert,' Martin announced, but he turned his face away as if he were ashamed of himself.

'I'll stay,' said Giuseppe, but he said it with a visible effort.

'And Jussi and François and Jean Pierre? And Nikolai?' asked Werner. He tried not to let them see how anxious he was for them to stay, but he dared not urge them. It was too dangerous here. Jussi was still badly shaken. He was crouched down on his knees in the snow sobbing quietly.

'Jussi must go back in any case,' Antti decided for him. 'He's got a brother and two sisters as well as a granny. I'm all on my own, so it's quite different for me. If I were you, Werner, I'd think twice about what you're doing. Don't forget you've still got a mother and father.'

'If other people hadn't gone on searching for my parents for fifty-six hours I should be an orphan like the rest of you. But I know what it feels like. I'm not going to leave Klaus in the lurch.' He did not look at anyone while he said this, not even at Klaus, because he was afraid they would see in his eyes how frightened he really was. Until a few days ago he had never been able to understand this terror of being buried under the snow, but now he knew what it was like and he was afraid.

He was not the only one. Paolo said in a small, high voice that was still rather unsteady:

'I'll stay too. I know you don't think much of me because I'm small and I'm as scared as a rabbit but I'm not going to run away. I'm as big as Klaus, anyway. Where are those tins of beans in tomato sauce?'

Everything seemed to have been flung about and half buried by the blast. Paolo began collecting loaves and tins of food together. The others took no notice. They were staring anxiously at François and Jean Pierre, who stood whispering and gesticulating at each other in rapid French. Nikolai stood by himself a little apart from the others. He had not made up his mind yet.

To lessen the tension Antti began to deal out more hunks of bread. Most of the boys began to eat mechanically. They were very hungry but they were so terribly thirsty as well.

At last the two French boys seemed to reach a decision.

'We're going to draw lots,' announced François. 'Jean Pierre wants to stay and I want to leave, but we're not going to be separated. Antti, break a piece of bread in two and hold the pieces behind your back. The biggest bit wins.'

Antti did as he asked and François won. That meant they would both go. The only one left now was Nikolai.

'Well,' he said slowly, 'I really wanted to go back too, but now there are so few of you staying, so ... well ... I'll stay too.'

Paolo sprang at him and gave him a huge hug. 'You're simply smashing, Nikolai. Gosh, I'd never have thought it of a Greek. Now everything's all right. The sun's come out and we've had something to eat. I bet the six of us will get on faster than when we were all getting in each other's way. Off with you!' And he waved away the five boys who stood ready to leave but still hesitating.

'Shut up, Paolo!' Antti ordered him sternly, while Holdert, whose face was white with pain, flung a look of fury at Paolo. 'After all, they've been working all night and Holdert didn't break his arm for fun.'

'I know,' murmured Paolo humbly. 'But they really must go now, they simply must, because if they don't I'm afraid I shall go with them after all,' he added uncomfortably.

The five boys turned and went. The others stared after them

with anxious faces – all except Paolo, who waved a snow shovel.

'Tell them to come and help us!' he shouted.

'Look, Jean Pierre and François are arguing with each other again,' he said a minute later to Werner and Antti, but they were already hard at work. Nikolai had grabbed a shovel too. Klaus had been burrowing away like a rabbit for some time.

'Oh well, the beans must wait,' muttered Paolo and began shovelling away the snow like mad. 'You're a fool, Paolo!' he thought to himself, 'the stupidest fool that ever was. You should have gone down with the others. In less than an hour you could have been snuggled down in bed with some nice hot coffee inside you. You could have been having a lovely snooze, dreaming of lemon trees in flower, all this time that you're digging away here like an idiot in this conf – in this beastly cold hard snow.'

He dug on wildly, hardly knowing what he was doing, too fagged out to control his movements, and suddenly he slithered down on to his knees in the deep trench. Raging with fury and despair he dug both hands into the snow, scraping away with all ten fingers till they were full of burning pain. Doubled up with his head on his knees he sobbed his heart out. In his helplessness he hammered with his clenched fists on the hard, close-packed snow till his knuckles were nearly skinned. The wild fit nearly made him faint. Everything went black before his eyes, he dug away wildly with his hands, boring into the snow with his arms.

'There are people buried here, people, *people!*' he murmured in a smothered voice. 'Do you hear that? *People!* You've buried them alive, you dirty, mean, beastly snow!'

He began talking to the snow, accusing it of all the wicked things it had done; this one small boy took up his stand against the forces of nature and the might of the mountains, all the powerful things that man alone is helpless against. And at the very moment when he was on the point of sobbing with helplessness as he felt himself broken by the ruthlessness of all this icy whiteness which held him in its grip, the fingers of his right hand felt something in the snow. It was something hard and angular. He tried to make the hole bigger with his hands, but got no farther. In a few short minutes its walls had frozen hard. He stood up with a jerk and grabbed his shovel. He did not say a word to the others. Bursting with excitement, he dug a hole above the place where he had felt something. Quite soon his shovel struck against wood. He went on digging and there it was. A corner where two beams joined. It looked as if it might be part of a torn-off roof.

Now at last he stood up. He was so far down that try as he would he could not see over the top of the trench. When he tried to shout he found he could not control his voice, only a queer little sound came from his dry, cracked lips. His throat felt as dry as leather.

With great difficulty he clambered up the side of the trench. When he reached the top he stayed there, sitting on his heels. He waved and shouted.

'I've found something! Klaus, Werner, Antti, come here!' His voice had lost all its uppishness.

The others looked up, surprised. They did not realize at first that he had said something important. Werner came over first. Klaus went on working as if he were deaf and blind. He looked quite bewildered when they fetched him over. But when he saw the uncovered timbers which might be the corner of a cow-house or a shed, he gave a sort of hoarse cry like an animal. He did not say a word but began digging away almost in a kind of stupor, while the others round him dug too. They found smashed and splintered wood. They found part of a roof that had been torn off and caved in. They found a thick beam with notches in it.

'It's the shed,' whispered Klaus so softly that they could hardly hear, 'it's not the cow-house.'

Hours ago Klaus had told them that his little sister Marie was in the shed.

They went on digging, but they felt that they were all in. Their breath came in great gasps which seemed to tear their chests. There was one moment when they believed they were there already, but slowly they grasped the fact that hours of work lay before them, work which perhaps they could not manage. The shed must not be allowed to cave in any further. If Marie were still alive that might kill her.

'We mustn't all stand here in a bunch,' said Antti warningly.

'I'm all in,' gasped Nikolai suddenly, flopping down like a sack of potatoes. Werner shook him but it was no good.

'Listen!' said Paolo suddenly. His voice was still only a hoarse whisper. 'Listen!'

They stood up and listened with heads raised. Someone was calling. A man's clear voice rang through the valley. 'Hallo-oh!'

'They're coming! They're *coming!*' Paolo exulted hoarsely.

Even Nikolai, who was lying quite still, opened his eyes at this. All the other boys climbed up on top of the heaps of snow which they had thrown up in the course of their digging. Their aching bodies were hardly able to stand upright. Slowly and painfully they stretched their stiff limbs and stared down the valley, straining their tired eyes.

'There!' cried Werner, pointing.

Far down the valley a row of black dots was slowly creeping up the slope towards them. It was the rescue squad, the men who were coming to take their place. They could hand the job over now.

Paolo flung himself on his knees. 'Oh dear Lord Jesus and all my granny's saints!' he stammered. 'Thank you! Oh, thank you!' He caught Antti's arm and pulled him down beside him. 'Pray, you beastly heathen!' he ordered fiercely. 'Pray that the poor little thing may still be alive!'

'Hallo-oh!' the voice from down the valley sounded again.

Werner slowly pulled off his cap and waved it to and fro. Behind him he heard Paolo say: 'Pray, you heathen!' Werner let his arm fall to his side and stood motionless. He wondered whether the burning, wordless wish which filled him could count as praying, but he didn't know.

12

MARIE

LITTLE Marie was carried out apparently uninjured from under the ruins of the shed. But the little body which the boys saw carried away by two of the soldiers looked so stiff and white and dead they could hardly believe it would ever come to life again.

Werner swallowed hard and Paolo, standing beside him, stared aghast at the still, waxen face with a bluish tinge on the closed eyelids, colourless lips, and dark plaits swinging as the men moved her.

'Why, she's pretty!' whispered Paolo.

Werner did not answer. Their success in finding the little girl filled him with such a confusion of feelings in which joy and sorrow were mixed that he could not say anything at all. Paolo, as usual, had no such difficulty.

Werner glanced at poor Klaus. Even before the soldiers had finished digging his sister out, he had suddenly heeled over without a sound. A medical orderly rolled him in blankets, laid him on a sledge and poured something between his lips, but it was no use. He lay unconscious like his sister amid the noise and movement of the rescue work.

Paolo, who had gone to sit on a sledge beside the exhausted Giuseppe, jumped up and stopped a passing medical orderly.

'Is she still alive?' he asked anxiously.

The man hesitated. He gave Paolo a long look and then asked:

'You're not the brother, are you?'

'No,' said Paolo.

'It's not certain yet that she's dead,' said the man.

Paolo nodded and went and sat down again.

The strain of the heavy work against time through the cold night hours had been too much for all the boys. Werner felt sick and was trembling all over. He looked down at Klaus, who lay warmly tucked up on his sledge, covered right up to his chin with grey blankets. The sun, softened by a thin veil of cloud, shone gently on his small sharp nose and bony looking forehead.

Beside him on a second sledge lay the big white nanny goat which had been dug out of the shed alive at the same time as Marie. The soldiers had wrapped the goat up in blankets as well, and bound her firmly on to the sledge. She lay there on her side, looking old and wise and patient. Her dirty white beard stuck out from under the blankets. Marie had been found lying between the goat's legs under a broken door which had shielded the two of them from the weight of the snow and given them enough air to breathe. She must have been milking the goat when the avalanche struck the shed.

'Perhaps she was able to suck some milk from his udders last night,' suggested Giuseppe, opening his eyes very wide as if he saw a miracle actually happening.

'*Her* udders, idiot!' said Paolo.

Giuseppe shrugged his shoulders. 'Oh, well –' he said absently.

Paolo's hands and knees were shaking with tiredness and the landscape was swimming before his eyes, but he kept up the grand manner to the end.

'In a few days' time we shall be back in school with old Pa Brandini, but I know I've forgotten everything I've ever learnt,' he said and added patronizingly: 'Poor old Brandini.'

But the others were not even listening.

Two soldiers who had been busy with a kind of miniature field kitchen came up to them with large aluminium mugs of steaming hot soup. The boys, who had so far had nothing to drink but some lukewarm tea out of someone's flask and whose mouths were still dry and parched, took it eagerly, but Werner's hands were shaking so much that he could hardly hold the mug. Most of the others had the same difficulty. Paolo slopped half of his in the snow.

'Stupid clot that I am!' he muttered fiercely and quickly drank up what was left, holding the mug in trembling hands.

The others drank their soup slowly, keeping their eyes on the group round Marie. They could not actually see her and they were forbidden to go any nearer. They were sent to the little camp near the field kitchen, where the sledges were and the equipment of the rescue squad and the little cupboard that was a field telephone.

First of all a medical orderly carefully examined all Marie's limbs and joints to see that nothing was broken. Then two teams of three men each took it in turns to give her artificial respiration. One of them squatted down on his knees astride her and moved regularly up and down, holding his large hands flat over her ribs and pressing them rhythmically. The other two moved her arms up and down, keeping time with the first. It seemed to be tiring work, for the men's faces were flushed and perspiring by the time the next men took over. A fourth man held her head on one side while a fifth and sixth were busy massaging her legs.

The boys stared in strained silence at the hard working group, as if they would drag Marie back to life simply with their eyes.

Once Paolo said hopefully: 'They wouldn't be trying so hard if there wasn't any hope.'

No one else said anything.

Over in the path of the avalanche the rest of the rescue party were working away, but they found no trace of Klaus and Marie's parents. The ground that they had searched yesterday was marked off with little green flags; it lay close to the path of the new avalanche that had fallen that morning. If yesterday's rescue party had worked straight on, there would have been accidents. Now the officer in charge sent his teams to sound more to the left, the thing that Klaus had urged in vain yesterday. The place where they had found the shed helped to fix the direction in which the cow-house must have been carried away.

The first search of the ground was carried out by men standing in a long row, as if for sounding but further apart. They found nothing, so the area was marked off with more green flags and the sounding began. Standing close together, the twenty men ran their sounding rods down into the deep snow.

'Now that's something like sounding rods,' whispered Paolo. 'Do you see that? They're as easy to handle as match sticks!'

They were light aluminium army sounding rods in six sections which screwed together. The men worked with easy, regular movements, thrusting the rods into the snow and pulling them out again. Now and then a man would test the joints of his rod. Words of command rang out in the stillness of the valley. The sun grew warmer. The rescue party worked on steadily, but they were depressed and gloomy. There was so little chance of finding Klaus and Marie's parents alive.

Werner glanced at Antti and Paolo. Antti kept dozing and waking up again and Paolo was trying to prop his eyes open in an effort to keep awake. Nikolai lay exhausted on a sledge. Giuseppe sat huddled up with his head on his arms; now and then he sighed, a long, quivering sigh.

Werner felt the sun warm on his back. For the first time for days the sky was really blue. The snow was thawing, and in these conditions a thaw was dangerous. The snow shone brilliantly in the sunlight. Luckily there was hardly any wind. Werner shook his head slowly like someone who cannot believe his eyes. It was all so improbable: the terrors of the last few days, the strain of this strange night. None of it seemed to fit the deceptive loveliness of the white peaks against the blue sky and the sunny peace of this upland valley. Here death walked abroad and the white terror still lurked.

Suddenly he heard an exclamation. The group of men round Marie stood up and one of them called out something. Another waved both arms in the air. Werner heard someone say: 'She's alive!'

He stood up and tried to go to them, but found he was trembling all over and had to sit down again. He clutched his head in both hands and shook it to and fro.

He heard Antti say: 'Do you think it helped? I'm glad you're seeing stars too.'

'She's alive! They've pulled it off! Did you hear?' yelled Paolo and staggered over to the sledge where Klaus was still lying motionless. Paolo began to shake him, first by the arm, then his shoulders, then his whole body.

'Klaus, Klaus!' he yelled in his ear. 'Your little sister's alive. Wake up and listen, can't you? She's alive!'

But Klaus gave no sign of life. A soldier watched them for a minute, then, seeing Paolo was very excited and overtired, he picked him up, carried him over to a sledge and wrapped him up in blankets.

'Now you lie there and be quiet,' he said, 'or we shall be having you on the sick list too, and we've enough on our hands as it is.'

Werner stumbled over to the group round Marie, which had now been joined by an officer. The men parted to let the boy through. He looked down gravely at the little girl. Her lips had a little colour in them now, her cheeks were not quite so white and she was breathing regularly, he could see that clearly, but her eyes were still shut and she seemed fast asleep.

She was quickly wrapped up in warm blankets. One of the medical orderlies poured something between her lips and she swallowed. Her eyelashes just quivered.

Werner felt a lump in his throat. He turned and walked away quickly. He was so full of thankfulness that he did not know what to do. He dawdled about among the untidy heaps of equipment. Now that the strain was over he found he was

so tired he could hardly stand. His arms and legs were stiff and hurt when he moved them and his mouth and throat were still dry with thirst. All the soup in the world would not be enough to quench it.

He wandered up to the soldier by the field telephone, who had been reporting progress at regular intervals and now passed on the good news to the rescue centre down in Brachen. Werner listened, lapping up every word.

'Rescue squad Snowdog at Valgretto here. Artificial respiration on eight-year-old Marie Watzig has been successful. Please have hospital bed ready. Internal injuries suspected. Great loss of blood. Ten men coming down with sledges. Request relief and dogs if available. Parents not yet found. Over.'

The telephonist scrabbled about with something in his little cupboard. Werner stood there quite still. The man looked up.

'What do you want?' he asked.

Werner tried to think what to say.

'Could you find out something for me from Brachen?' he asked timidly.

'What d'you want to know?'

'Well, I should awfully like to know whether my friend has broken his arm or not,' Werner explained.

The man looked at him with an expression which Werner could not understand.

'Eleven of us came up here last night,' he explained. 'Early in the morning five of them went back. One had hurt his arm. We were afraid it might be broken.'

The soldier still stared at him without answering. His young face was tanned and his eyes were the bluest that Werner had ever seen. But there was a queer expression in them which he could not fathom.

'Well I'm blowed,' the soldier said at last. 'You mean to say eleven of you young idiots were crazy enough to come up here, risking your necks and never thinking of the peck of trouble you'd make for us if anything went wrong, eh?'

Werner turned crimson. He didn't know what to say. He just stared at the man.

'Oh well, it's that sort of daftness that makes the world go round,' the man went on, 'blessed young idiots that you are. You deserve a good hiding, all the lot of you, but you've probably saved that child's life.' He nodded towards where Marie lay. 'We may even get the parents out, you never know. The craziest things have been happening these last few days. You find a man dead after being buried five minutes under the snow. Others are still alive after being buried for days. At Urteli they dug out a couple alive after fifty-six hours.'

Werner began to laugh helplessly. He was so tired that he could not stop but just laughed and laughed, his shoulders heaving as he stood facing the soldier and hiccoughing with laughter, going on and on weakly till he suddenly felt he wanted to lean helplessly on the man's shoulder and laugh and cry at the same time. And that, of course, was one of the things a boy did not do. Paolo might do it, but Paolo never gave the impression of being a real boy. Or was he? He had stayed to go on with the digging, though he admitted being the most frightened of them all. And didn't that make him the bravest?

Young idiots the soldier had called them, and talked about a peck of trouble – a good hiding – young idiots. But Marie was being brought back to life at this very moment. She had the longest, darkest plaits he had ever seen on a pale-faced little girl. Plaits like that ought to be swinging in the wind as she danced along. And the soldier knew of a couple at Urteli who had been dug out alive after fifty-six hours. And here was he, Werner, standing and laughing with a lump in his throat, laughing and laughing and could not stop . . .

'Now then!' the soldier grasped his shoulders and gave him a good shaking. 'What's up with you, for goodness sake? Gone off your chump?'

Werner let himself be shaken limply to and fro. It was a pleasant feeling. Everything comes to those who wait –

everything – all mixed up together like this and then back in its proper place.

'Oy!' shouted the soldier in his ear. 'Didn't you want to know if one of your friends has broken his arm? I'll find out.'

Oh yes, of course, Holdert. . . . Werner felt the man let go his shoulders. He stood there for a few seconds, then everything went black before his eyes and he fell in a heap in the snow.

13

WHERE DO WE GO FROM HERE?

WHEN he came to, he was lying on his camp bed in the station restaurant at Brachen. It was broad daylight and only one or two people here and there were sitting or lying on their beds. The place seemed less full than before. He looked at the corner over by the coffee machines to see if Klaus were lying there, but the bed had been taken away.

He looked round slowly. He had a queer, light-headed feeling and wondered how long he had been asleep.

Paolo was in the next bed. He was asleep, but his hands moved restlessly on the coverlet and now and then he muttered something. Further along Nikolai and Giuseppe lay fast asleep.

The camp beds of the others had been tidily made. They were empty. The boys must have gone off to the village.

Werner raised himself on one elbow and gave a little grunt of pain. All his muscles hurt. He looked round a bit further. Then he saw Hans Peter sitting behind him a little way away. He was sitting on a pile of knapsacks between two beds with his back against the wall, staring gloomily before him. Werner beckoned, but Hans Peter did not see. He was sunk in thought.

Would he be angry at their having gone off without him? He would have been a great help, but he could never have given Mr Hutamäki the slip like the rest of them. Would he know how Klaus and Marie were? And whether their parents had been found?

Werner heaved himself up a bit farther and all his muscles seemed to protest. He was aching everywhere – back, shoulders, arms.

'Hans Peter!' he said in an urgent whisper.

Hans Peter jumped. He stood up rather reluctantly and came over to Werner's bed.

'How do you feel?' he asked gruffly.

'I'm fine. How are the others?'

'I've been left here as watchdog,' said Hans Peter. 'You're none of you to get up till the doctor says you may. He's coming back this afternoon. There was no room for you in hospital.'

'But there's nothing wrong with us!' exclaimed Werner in surprise.

Hans Peter did not answer.

'How long have we been asleep?' asked Werner.

'Two nights and a day and a half.'

Werner's jaw dropped.

'They gave you injections to make you sleep. You were suffering from exhaustion or something. The doctor said Nikolai was sinking, whatever that may be. They made quite a song and dance about you.'

'But I feel fine,' protested Werner. 'My muscles ache a bit, that's all.'

Hans Peter shrugged his shoulders. 'Well, you looked pretty mouldy, all the lot of you, when they brought you in here the day before yesterday. You all had jabs at the hospital. You looked more dead than alive, I can tell you, and Hutamäki had the scare of his life. He's had a long pow-wow by telephone with the Head of our village. He was nearly off his chump. And it was a mean trick you played us, creeping out while we were asleep instead of taking us with you.'

'We couldn't help that,' said Werner. 'Mr Hutamäki would never have approved of your coming and you might have let on to him about us.'

'Honestly, I don't know what I should have done,' Hans Peter admitted. He was not so gruff now. 'But I've never been so angry in all my life.'

Werner glanced over to the corner where he had expected

to see Klaus. He hesitated and then asked: 'Do you know how Klaus and his sister are?'

Hans Peter looked uncomfortable. He began to say something and then stopped, looking away so as not to meet Werner's eyes.

'D'you mean it was all for nothing?' Werner asked suddenly with his heart in his mouth.

Hans Peter shook his head. 'Marie's alive, but they don't know if she'll pull through.' He paused. 'And they've found the parents, they were both dead.' He paused again and it was a minute before he added, 'And Klaus is very ill. He's delirious.'

Werner felt the blood beating in his temples. His heart was thumping. He felt dizzy and lay down again on his back. He stared at the ceiling, which had Alpine flowers carved on it. Hans Peter sat down in silence on the floor between his bed and Paolo's.

'Everyone here is getting on fine,' Hans Peter went on presently in a flat, expressionless voice. 'Bartel Gurtnelli's parents are getting better. And Bartel has been lent a chess-board and some chessmen by one of the doctors in the hospital and he's teaching Old John to play chess. Your Aunt Augusta has been spending half her time in the flat above with her cats. She helped with Mrs Rähmi's baby when it had to be rushed into hospital with appendicitis. And that English girl you made friends with is looking after the little Rähmi boy.' He looked round the almost empty room. 'But most of them are out now. It's visiting time at the hospital. And the trains are running again. A lot of the tourists and evacuees have left.'

But Werner was not listening any more. His head felt a bit swimmy. He could see Klaus, and Marie's pinched white face. Oughtn't he and the other boys to have done what they did? Had they just been crazy fools?

Then he remembered Klaus as he was when he was brought

in that evening, sobbing and kicking because he had had to
leave the place where his parents were buried. He had shouted
out things and no one had listened to him. He had known they
had been searching in the wrong place. They were not far out
and of course the grown-ups thought they could point out the
exact spot where the shed and the cow-house had stood better
than a small boy. ... In his helplessness there was nothing
Klaus could do but howl. But later he had dug like blazes. He
had hardly been like a human boy at all, more like a rabbit or
a badger.

And had all they had done been wrong? Were they just a
pack of crack-brained children? Had they just caused more
misery? Klaus was delirious, his parents were dead after all,
and Marie. ...

'What exactly is wrong with Marie?' he asked.

Hans Peter hesitated, but after a bit he answered.

'She's bled an awful lot inside,' he said. 'She's got to have an
operation. They wanted to do it yesterday afternoon but they
couldn't because they hadn't any blood for her.'

'No blood?' asked Werner, puzzled.

'She's got to have a blood transfusion before the operation,
and after it's over. But they hadn't the right kind of blood.
They couldn't find anyone that had exactly the same kind of
blood as she has. As a rule it isn't so tricky, but with Marie it
was very difficult. They had to have someone belonging to a
particular blood group and usually they have plenty of people
to choose from, but this time they hadn't. Mr Hutamäki told
me about it. It was something about serum and something
about unsuccessful cross-checks – all very complicated. A lot of
us went over to let them test our blood. They tried me and Mr
Hutamäki and Bartel. But our blood wasn't good enough
either. There were two doctors and three nurses working on
us and they were all a bit snappy with us because word kept on
coming up from the lab. that it still wasn't the right kind of
blood and from the operating theatre to say there was no

time to waste. And you'll never guess who had the right kind in the end.'

'Who?' demanded Werner excitedly.

'Your Aunt Augusta. First they wouldn't try her. They said she was too old and her blood pressure wasn't high, or something. They tried Old John, but his blood wouldn't do.'

'So they had to have hers after all?'

'She was so cross with the doctors when they wouldn't try her that they gave in. And then they found she had exactly the right kind. Blood group O, Rhesus negative. Ever heard of it?' asked Hans Peter.

Werner shrugged. What did he care about all these strange long words?

'Well, what happened?' he asked. 'Were they in time?'

'I'm not quite sure about what happened after that. They took Aunt Augusta away with them and we were all thanked and sent back here. It was an awful disappointment for Old John.'

'And have they operated on her?'

'Yesterday evening, but they don't know yet if it's been successful or not. It should have been done much sooner. Old John and his wife have gone to see your aunt. She had to stay in hospital.'

Werner lay quite still on his back. It was all too much for him to take in at once. Aunt Augusta and Marie . . . it was all so wonderful. He knew just what his father would have said about it: 'It was meant.'

He tried to think. If he and his father had not fetched the boys down from the hut above Urteli, they would not have been evacuated together. If they had not come here to Brachen, Klaus would not have been able to take them up to his home. In that case Marie would be dead by now, for she could only have lasted a couple of hours longer. And if Aunt Augusta had not been evacuated with them she would not have been able to give her blood. It was meant. . . .

But then, what about the avalanches? Were they meant, too? That could not be right. There must be something wrong somewhere. All those people killed and injured, all that grief and suffering. . . . His whole heart revolted against the idea of so much pain. It was senseless for the snow to come hurtling down from the mountains. It was dreadful that nature should be able to make people small and frightened and unhappy. But why did it happen, then? Why? Why? Why did Klaus and Marie have to lose their father and mother?

'*I* don't know,' he muttered suddenly half aloud.

'What is it?' asked Hans Peter. 'What don't you know?'

'Why do all these things happen? Why can't people just live happy and ordinary lives?'

'Happy and ordinary isn't the same,' said Hans Peter slowly. 'I believe you're only happy if you *know* you're happy. And you only know that after you've been miserable. A lot of us in the children's village have learned that.'

Werner said nothing. Hans Peter went on rather uncertainly:

'The Head of our village told us something once. He said misfortune shakes you awake and you've all had a jolly good shaking up and are wide awake, but it's only when you're awake that life becomes quite real, because you've learned what it's worth.' As Werner still said nothing, Hans Peter added shyly, 'It sounds a bit like a sermon.'

'Sermon? What sermon? Sermons are always frightfully boring!' said Paolo's voice suddenly. He had woken up and was staring at them round-eyed. Without waiting for an answer he went on, 'I've never had such a gorgeous sleep in my life before. One smashing dream after another. Pity I'm awake now and can see your faces. It's a come-down, I can tell you.'

Werner and Hans Peter exchanged looks. They smiled and felt years older.

'Turn over on your other side,' Hans Peter suggested. 'P'raps you'll go to sleep again.'

'I'm awake and I'm going to stay awake,' declared Paolo. 'What's the time and where are the others? How are Klaus and his sister getting on and have they –?' He broke off and looked uncertainly from one face to the other. Some of the truth dawned on him before either said anything. He went rather pale, turned over with his back to them and lay perfectly still. It was as if Paolo were not Paolo any more.

'But Marie's alive,' whispered Hans Peter bending over him.

'I should hope so, too!' came Paolo's smothered voice from under the bedclothes.

★

The visitors, however, brought back good news from the hospital. Marie was a little better and Aunt Augusta, though weak after giving nearly two pints of blood, was getting on splendidly.

'And a beef steak for her dinner,' Old John told them, 'though she couldn't quite finish it. And now she calls herself a Donor. That's a fine word. It's Latin and means that you've given your blood. Well, fancy my living to be jealous of Augusta Altschwank!'

That evening Werner and Paolo were given permission to visit Aunt Augusta. They had a strange, light feeling in their heads as they strode through the streets. The snow, which had thawed during the day till it was like thick porridge, had frozen again and crackled under their feet.

When they got to the hospital they were taken straight to Aunt Augusta, and to their great surprise and delight they found Marie lying in the next bed. Everything in the big ward was white, the walls, beds and bedspreads, and against all this whiteness her still face showed some colour. She lay with her eyes closed and her hands under the coverlet. Her long dark plaits lay one on each side of her. She looked just like a doll.

'You boys aren't looking at me at all,' complained Aunt Augusta's voice sharply.

Werner and Paolo looked. They had expected to see Aunt Augusta's familiar face, but this pale, friendly, wrinkled creature was not a bit like the Aunt Augusta they remembered. Her voice still had the old snappish tone but her eyes twinkled and her mouth did not seem such a hard straight line as it used to.

'Hullo, Auntie,' said Werner shyly.

Paolo felt in his pocket and pulled out a rather crumpled but quite clean and fairly presentable handkerchief.

'It isn't much, but it's with my love,' he announced, dumping his gift on the bed with a flourish.

'That's a boy's handkerchief,' said the old lady turning pink with pleasure.

'Your nose won't notice that,' Paolo assured her.

'I've never had a present from a boy before,' said Aunt Augusta. 'This must be my second girlhood.' She laughed at her own joke. Then she looked across at Marie. 'Isn't she pretty?' she said. 'Have you ever seen such a pretty little girl? And she's getting on. The doctor's very pleased with her.' Her voice had dropped to a whisper. 'She's alive now because she's had some of my blood. Did you know that?'

The boys nodded without a word. They thought Marie was alive because they had found her in the snow.

'She'll be well again in a few weeks,' the old lady went on. 'But she has no father and mother now and no home. I thought she might come and live with me when my house is built up again. It's very healthy air up at Urteli. She can have a little room of her own and then she can stay with me always.'

At the back of his mind Werner seemed to hear his father saying to his mother: 'Poor old Aunt Augusta; her trouble is she's all alone.'

He stared at his queer old aunt. He had never seen her look like this before. She leaned back proudly against her pillows and looked happy. She felt that now she would not be alone for the rest of her life. She looked on the little girl as her own child, but Werner looked at her too and felt uncertain.

'I'm going to have my house built up again just as it was before,' he heard Aunt Augusta say. 'And later she can help me in the shop and we'll save up for her trousseau. I'll give her a very nice trousseau.'

Werner seemed to see Marie's little face floating like a white speck about Aunt Augusta's shop. He felt afraid. He was not sure if it would be a good thing for Marie to come and live up in Urteli with Aunt Augusta and save up for her trousseau. He glanced at Paolo for support, but Paolo was absorbed in watching Marie's face on the pillow.

'You know Snow White that people make such a fuss about,' he said. 'I don't believe she was any prettier than Marie. I wonder what she'll look like when she wakes up.'

'I've seen her awake,' whispered Aunt Augusta. 'She was awake when they brought her in here.'

'She really ought to stay with Klaus,' said Paolo innocently.

'I've no room for a boy,' snapped Aunt Augusta at once. 'Boys are a nuisance. But a nice little girl like this –'

'I missed my brothers and sisters very much,' said Paolo, looking her straight in the eyes. 'I had five of them – and I'm the only one left. My granny tried to comfort me, but she knew why I cried so much. If I hadn't gone to the children's village –'

Aunt Augusta had bright red patches on her cheeks. She moved her hands as if she were pushing something away.

'You won't talk me into taking the boy as well. He's got a grandmother and grandfather at Appenzell. He can go to them.'

'Then Marie must go there too,' said Paolo in a voice which was so unexpectedly quiet for him that Werner was astonished. Aunt Augusta blinked and her hands moved nervously. Werner was sorry for her.

'Perhaps the grandparents can take only one,' he said. 'Not many people can suddenly take in two extra children.'

Paolo's eyes flashed. 'You don't know what you're talking about!' he declared.

'I'm alone at home too,' said Werner.

'You've never had brothers and sisters!'

'If Marie comes to Urteli, I shall be there too,' he answered illogically.

A nurse came up to them on silent feet. Her starched apron rustled.

'You boys are forgetting you're in a hospital,' she admonished them in a whisper. 'You can squabble outside. Visiting time is nearly over, anyway.'

Werner flushed to the roots of his hair and took two steps backwards, but Paolo, unabashed, hugged Aunt Augusta and kissed her on both cheeks till her glasses hung askew on her nose.

'I've always said you were like my granny,' he beamed, 'all prickles outside and as soft as toasted cheese underneath. P'raps you'll think it over.'

But when the boys had left the ward Aunt Augusta shook her old head obstinately.

'Boys get on my nerves, they always have, and that Klaus won't be any better than the others,' she grumbled. 'Marie is a girl, a dear, biddable little girl and I gave nearly two pints of my blood to save her life. If it weren't for me she wouldn't be here now. I've got a child of my own at last. And I shall look after her far better than her own mother.'

'You must try and get some sleep,' said the nurse, coming back. 'It isn't good for you to get excited.'

'Boys,' repeated Aunt Augusta, 'boys get on my nerves, they always have. But that little dark, curly haired one isn't at all bad for a boy.' She picked up the handkerchief that was lying on her bed and blew her nose quite unnecessarily.

★

The boys walked together through the long corridors.

'You upset Aunt Augusta,' said Werner.

Paolo looked up at him earnestly. 'Look here, Werner,' he said, 'we got Marie out of the snow. Now we're responsible for what becomes of her.' He slapped his chest. 'I feel like a sort of – well – a sort of godfather.'

'She's got plenty of godfathers, then!' laughed Werner.

'Ten,' agreed Paolo promptly. 'That's quite all right. But you and I are the most important. We should never have pulled it off at all without you, and I found her.'

'It may not be so bad if she comes to Urteli,' said Werner slowly. 'Aunt Augusta will look after her very nicely and we can keep an eye on her too.' He did not take the business so seriously as Paolo, and to be quite frank he rather looked forward to Marie coming there. Of course she would miss Klaus, but would it really be as bad as Paolo made out?

Walking along the corridor towards them was a doctor in a long white coat. He glanced at them sharply and then stopped and said:

'Aren't you the boys who helped dig out the Watzig child?'

'Yes, sir.'

The doctor had a good look at them. 'You're looking better now than you did the evening I gave you an injection. Did you have a good sleep?'

While he talked to them he seemed to be thinking of something else. He ran his eyes over them and then looked past them at a little red lamp that burned above one of the doors.

'I handed you two over to my assistant, but Klaus Watzig is my patient,' he said. 'He isn't getting on as well as I should like. Will you come and see him? I think it may do him good. He may recognize you.'

They followed the doctor.

Klaus lay in a little room all by himself. He had changed so much they hardly knew him. His little face was thin and sunken and his nose stuck out in a sharp point. His eyes were half open and only the whites showed.

Werner and Paolo stood at the end of the bed and stared down appalled at the unconscious Klaus.

'He's quiet now,' the nurse said to the doctor, who was standing behind the two boys, 'but he's been wandering again. All about a goat that ran away into the forest and he had to fetch her back. She would jump up the rocks and over clefts where he couldn't follow.'

The doctor nodded.

He looked at the two boys, 'Now listen,' he said. 'There's nothing to worry about. He'll get better, I promise you that. But he's suffering from shock and nervous strain. It wasn't an easy job up there that night, was it? But you got the little girl out safely and that's the main thing. Now there's something I think you can do for Klaus. All this business has upset him rather so that he has – well, you might say he's run away into the past. But he's had a scare in the past too. What nurse was just telling me is probably something that frightened him badly when he was quite little. He's dreaming about it now although he's awake. But he's got to come back into the present, do you understand? And you may be able to help. If he recognizes you, that'll be a great step forward. He must see your faces and hear your voices. Have you got on the same clothes as you had on then?'

They nodded.

'Go and stand close to him at the head of the bed and say some of the things to him that you said that night.' He saw them hesitate and said firmly, 'Yes, I know it isn't easy, but have a shot at it. And don't be afraid if he gets restless, it won't be easy for him, you know. He'll be afraid and think he's back in the night of the avalanche. But that doesn't matter, he's got to face it. What he's been through is much worse than that.'

Paolo went up to him rather uncertainly. 'Klaus!' he called.

'Klaus! How much farther is it now?' His voice was high and shrill with nervousness. His hands felt clammy. 'Klaus!' he called again louder. 'Klaus, is it very much farther to Valgretto?'

Klaus's eyelids quivered, his eyes opened a little more and his whole body trembled.

The doctor gave Werner a little nudge.

'Klaus!' said Werner, but his voice was so gruff it could hardly be heard. He cleared his throat and tried again. 'Klaus! It's me, Werner. Take your boots and come with me. You've got to show us the way up to your home. We're going to get Marie out of the snow and you've got to show us the way. Klaus, there are eleven of us, counting you. Get out of bed and bring your boots!'

Werner was holding his fists tightly clenched. He could hardly bear to see the scared expression on Klaus's face. The boy moaned and began to thresh about with his arms. He flung himself over on his other side. 'I daren't !' he cried.

'Klaus!' Paolo called again. 'Here's your stick. We're going to search. Where is the shed?'

'I won't! I won't!' moaned Klaus, frightened.

'Klaus, we've found the corner of the shed. Here's a shovel! Come and dig! You won't get anywhere grubbing with your hands. Here's the hole. We're digging it bigger. D'you see? I say, Klaus! They're coming to help us! Soldiers, Klaus!'

Klaus grew so restless that Werner and Paolo glanced anxiously at the doctor, but he nodded reassuringly. 'That's right. Now let him see your faces. Go nearer.'

'Klaus!' Paolo called shrilly and bent over so that his face was just above him. Klaus opened his eyes wide. He stared at Paolo and whimpered:

'Not alone! I don't want to be left alone!'

'You're not alone,' said Paolo clearly. 'We're here with you, helping. It's going along fine.'

Klaus still stared at him wide-eyed. His pupils were strangely large and black. 'Don't leave me alone! Promise!' he begged.

'I promise,' said Paolo solemnly.

'Where are the others?' whispered Klaus.

Paolo pulled Werner forward. 'Here's Werner,' he said.

'She will keep jumping away,' whimpered Klaus, 'and it's getting so dark.'

Deeply disappointed the two boys looked round at the doctor, who nodded slowly.

'Not too bad,' he said. 'He's still confusing the night with you and that business with the goat. It'll come all right. I'm glad I ran into you. Can you come back tomorrow morning? Bring a couple of the others with you if you can.'

'We're going back to the children's village tomorrow,' said Paolo doubtfully. 'The trains to Zurich are running again.'

'Then ask the teacher in charge of you to ring me up this evening,' said the doctor. 'I'm here till ten.' He went with them as far as the entrance. 'I know it was a difficult job,' he said again, 'but you were a lot of help.'

Werner and Paolo walked down the steep, narrow little streets near the station in silence, haunted by the picture of Klaus's frightened face in the big hospital bed.

'And when he wakes up properly they'll have to tell him that his mother and father are dead and that he's going to live with his grandparents,' said Paolo gloomily. 'I only hope his granny's a bit like mine!'

'He'll be awfully happy to see Marie again,' said Werner softly.

Paolo gripped Werner's arm and stopped dead so suddenly that his feet nearly slid from under him. Werner grabbed him quickly and Paolo swung round and thrust his face close to his.

'Ah, now you're talking!' he said. 'You're beginning to see that those two must be together, aren't you? We simply can't let them down. We've got to go on helping them. Only I don't know how. You heard how Klaus kept whimpering

"Don't leave me alone! Don't leave me alone!" – He'll get well again soon and come out of hospital, but you needn't tell me he'll be cured of that fear. It stays and stays for years. I've had it too – I get it still – when I least expect it, it grips hold of me again. You don't know what it meant to me, that first day, when you grabbed my hand under the snow and didn't let go. No one in the world could have done more for me. You're three parts idiot and one part saint, but my granny says the really good people always are.'

Two or three people in the street stopped to stare at the excited boy, shouting and waving his arms in the air. Werner felt embarrassed. He gave Paolo a push and said quietly:

'You needn't use your arms and legs to talk with. And anyway you said I was a stuffed dummy.'

'So you are!' said Paolo. 'What's more, you're absolutely clueless, but I admit you've had your wits about you a bit more the last couple of days.'

Werner remembered what Hans Peter had said about trouble shaking you awake. He had been frightfully miserable for those few days. But his next words had nothing to do with that.

'What I should like to know is how old you really are,' he said.

'Nosey!' retorted Paolo. 'And it's the same sickening question the grown-ups always ask when they can't think of anything else to say. Oh well, all right, I'll tell you. I'm fourteen and three months, but no one will ever believe it. I bet you aren't much older yourself.'

'I'm 15,' said Werner. 'I shall be 16 in the spring.'

'Terrific!' jeered Paolo. 'But you're only a big child for all that.'

Werner looked down from his five foot eight on the little Italian.

'That's what I think about you when you make so much fuss about nothing,' he observed.

Paolo shrugged. 'My granny says it's in the blood. It's our temperament. Like a fish being deaf or a pig squealing. My father kept a stall in the market and he made a living for his wife and six children by his chatter. Half the time he talked in verse – he'd taught himself to do that – and my eldest brother was called Dante and was to have been a student. Sometimes I feel I must make as much noise as the six of us would have made if the others'd been still alive.' Paolo stamped on a frozen lump of snow and smashed it. When Werner said nothing he burst out: 'Klaus and Marie ought to come to the children's village. And you ought to come and get a job with us. Hans Peter's going away; he's going to be apprenticed to a cabinet maker at St Gall. You might put in for his job. You've been working for a carpenter, haven't you?'

Werner shook his head.

'Can't be done,' he said. 'Father and Mother will need me. And Marie's going to Aunt Augusta. And the children's village is only for war orphans, anyway.'

'Oh no, not only them,' said Paolo. 'Supplies are running out, I'm glad to say. Klaus and Marie could go to the Polish house because the Poles have all gone now and Swiss orphans are coming there instead.'

Werner began to lengthen and quicken his stride, a sign that he was thinking hard. He was thinking of tomorrow when he must say good-bye to them all. He found he could not imagine life without them. He would miss Paolo in particular, for they had become real friends, and Werner did not make friends easily.

'It's all very nice, what you've planned,' he said gruffly, 'but you aren't in charge.'

'And I'm not an ostrich either!' panted Paolo. 'For heaven's sake don't walk so fast!'

They had nearly reached the station. The snow in the street in front of it looked dirty in the white light of an arc lamp.

'Anyway it was a crazy idea,' said Werner, hoping to be contradicted. But for once in his life Paolo did not contradict.

'Oh well, I just thought it might be nice,' said he in a quiet voice that quivered a little.

Werner looked round in surprise.

'I'd like to smash the beastly train to bits!' cried Paolo suddenly. 'I think it's absolute rot that we aren't to see each other again after tomorrow!'

'I'll save up and come and visit you at the children's village,' Werner promised. 'And when I come I'll bring Marie with me.'

THE CHILDREN'S VILLAGE

'THAT isn't a bouquet, it's simply a mess,' said a little girl whose real name was Sylvia but who was called Tishoo because she was always sneezing. Especially now that the hay was cut. She was a jolly little girl and she and Paolo were well matched. After sneezing thirteen times in succession she would look very doleful, but a minute later she would be laughing again.

'It makes me so tired,' she explained. 'But there's no reason why you shouldn't have a good laugh out of it. I should think it funny myself if it wasn't me.'

At this moment Tishoo stood facing Paolo with a face of thunder. 'It's simply nothing like a bouquet,' she said awfully, 'it's just a *mistake!*'

Paolo looked at it. He had done his best, but possibly sunflowers, geraniums, and everlasting pea did not go frightfully well together.

'Come on,' cried Tishoo, 'let's go and pick all the wild flowers we can find. P'raps we can shove these things of yours in among them.'

'We haven't much time,' objected Paolo.

'Oh, rot, we've loads,' declared Tishoo and darted ahead. Instead of following the track downhill she chose a narrow little track leading upwards. The tall grass round the field was full of flowers, and further up lay a meadow sprinkled with camomile and late campanulas. They set to work, Tishoo picking flowers and sneezing alternately, and Paolo picking flowers and every now and then raising his head to listen. This was nonsense, of course, because they would not be able to hear the little train for ages. He had worked it all out and the train could only just have left St Gall, but he had no head for figures and he was impatient all the same.

Tishoo, with her arms full of flowers, was seized with an appalling fit of sneezing.

'Here, give them to me!' cried Paolo, snatching them from her so that half of them fell to the ground. He picked them up while she went on sneezing. The tears streamed down her face.

'I think it's perfectly ridiculous that they haven't found a cure for hay fever,' he observed severely.

'Don't go! It's coming on again!' gasped Tishoo between two sneezing fits.

'Come on!' called Paolo and turned back to the little path that led down to the village.

At the turn of the path that led past the children's houses the others were waiting for them. Antti and Jussi were there and Jean Pierre with two little French girls who wanted to come too. Holdert and Martin had not been able to get away because they were setting up the type for the village newspaper and could not take the time off to go down to Trogen. But Giuseppe and Nikolai were there, and the teacher at the head of the Austrian house was coming with two of his children because he had an errand to do at Trogen.

'Aren't you two ever coming?' called Antti impatiently.

'Oh, don't lose your wool!' shouted Paolo and the others laughed.

'Oh, yeah? I know someone who was up and cleaning his teeth by five o'clock this morning!' began Giuseppe, quite prepared to tell tales out of school.

The Austrian teacher, in a check shirt and leather shorts and with a little girl clinging to each hand, had gone on in front.

Trogen lay below them with its little railway station, its black church steeple, its roofs and gardens. When they reached the first houses, Paolo was too impatient to keep with the others. He plunged down a steep, narrow little path that branched off to the right, while the others turned left along the broader track. They had plenty of time.

Tishoo glanced uncertainly from the crowd of boys and girls on the wider path to the dark hole between the bushes where Paolo had vanished. Then she followed the others. She felt rather important today because Paolo had chosen her for a momentous part. He had been afraid there would be only boys meeting the visitors at the train and he did not feel that was right.

'Look here, Tishoo,' he had said, 'there's a little girl called Marie coming with my friend. You can tell the little ones in your house' (Tishoo lived in the Greek house) 'that she looks like Snow White and the Seven Dwarfs. She has black hair in two plaits and blue eyes – at least, I believe they're blue, I've never seen them open. And she's all alone, so she needs a little friend and you'll do just nicely, Tishoo.' He had looked at her with his most charming smile and Tishoo had allowed herself to be roped in. Of course, you could never be sure with Paolo that all he said was true, but she believed him this time, something in his tone impressed her. It was serious and matter-of-fact and unaffected – and Paolo was not often like that.

They still had to wait seven minutes on the little station platform before the train, which consisted of an engine and one light blue coach, crept slowly round the corner. Paolo, with his big bunch of flowers in his hand, stood in front between Antti and Tishoo who, conscious of the important part she had to play, had stepped forward perkily, to the annoyance of Jean Pierre and Giuseppe, who thought she had no business there.

'Don't you take any notice of what they say,' Paolo whispered quickly.

Tishoo was an independent-spirited young lady and already had vast experience behind her when she landed in an orphanage in Athens at the age of six. She nodded reassuringly. She was not afraid of rude remarks from a pack of boys, and that was the worst that could happen to you in the children's village. At the last moment she picked a few flowers out of Paolo's bunch so as not to stand there empty-handed.

The little train drew up and people got out. The group of waiting children stared in suspense. Were they never coming?

Suddenly Werner was there. A bit taller and in a brand new suit, flushed and shy, he came up to the children in their faded, practical country clothes.

'But where's Marie?' asked Paolo, grasping the flowers firmly against his chest.

'She couldn't come,' said Werner rather uncomfortably.

'Why not?' demanded Paolo fiercely.

Werner's eyes wandered helplessly over the reception committee and said: 'That's what I want to talk about.'

Tishoo stared at him, her face blank with disappointment which she made no attempt to conceal, and stuffed her bunch of flowers into his hands.

'I'm Sylvia Nikomenides. I want to make friends with Marie.'

'That's off for the moment,' said Paolo, stuffing his great bunch of flowers into her hands. He really could not hand them to Werner himself. It simply wasn't done.

The boys crowded round Werner, asking him so many questions that he had no time to get a word in edgeways. They wanted to know everything about the friends at Urteli. Were his father and mother all right now? How was Aunt Augusta? Had the houses been built up again? Had they got more cows? Was Marie perfectly fit again now?

The Austrian teacher pushed through the crowd and shook hands with Werner. The little Austrian girls made little curtsies, the short plaits of one of them dancing as she bobbed.

'Welcome to our village, Werner. Mr Hutamäki sends his best wishes. He was sorry not to come and meet you himself. He had to go to a meeting at St Gall, so I came instead. But he'll be back before you leave this evening.'

Werner looked disappointed. He particularly wanted to have a talk with Mr Hutamäki about Marie, and that was not going to be easy if he saw him for only a few minutes. Werner now hoped to get Paolo to himself as soon as possible.

But this was not easy. Jostled by the whole troop of happy, boisterous children, he walked up the mountain. Tishoo, who had not got Marie to look after, kept close beside him. He glanced sideways at her. She looked a nice child, happy and carefree, the very opposite of Marie. He chuckled at the idea of Paolo organizing this friendship between the two little girls beforehand without even knowing how badly it was needed.

The last houses were behind them now, light-coloured stone houses with sunny windows and little gardens full of flowers and shrubs. The road went on upwards between fields, on the left lay a rambling old farm house with a dog which started barking violently and a yard full of junk, where an old farmer was just taking a horse out of the shafts. He called good day to the children and they all called back to him cheerfully. 'Be quiet, Towser!' he shouted at the dog.

'Oh, let him bark, we're not afraid of him!' laughed one of the little French girls who had come with Jean Pierre. She was a tall child with fair plaits and looked German rather than French. She spoke both languages equally well and had been five years at the children's village.

The more Werner looked at the children running along beside him the more determined he was to fight tooth and nail to get Marie into the school. Paolo would be able to tell him what must be done; it had been Paolo's idea in the first place, when Werner had thought that she would be all right at Urteli.

He did not really know quite what had gone wrong. He could see that she was pale and shy and he could understand that she was homesick. But he would never have believed that the little group of children in his own village, where everyone was poor and worked hard for a living, could be surly and stand-offish. The temporary schoolmaster who was taking Hans Altschwank's place till Whitsun had done his best, but he had not succeeded in breaking down the barrier. The little orphan from Valgretto remained a shy, lonely stranger.

Werner had been away from Urteli for quite a long time. While his father and mother were in hospital he had lived with an uncle and aunt in Zurich. He had taken a three-months course as an electrician and worked very hard. He had only got back in the spring. The Altschwanks' new house was almost finished by then and he had helped the workmen, who were from another village, for a few weeks. The village hardly recognized him. Werner had not grown talkative but his old tongue-tied shyness had gone.

'Now he's seen the world,' said Regli, his former boss, shaking his head. 'He won't stay long in Urteli now. You mark my words.'

Regli was always predicting something, though he usually got it wrong. But this time he was right. Werner wanted to go.

'Well, good luck, my boy,' his father had said to him yesterday, when Werner set off on his journey to Trogen. 'And remember, you're not going for yourself alone but for Marie, too. Here's a letter to the Head of the children's village. It may not do any good but it can't do any harm.'

His mother gave him a large packet of sandwiches filled with Finetti's best sausage.

'You must go and work where there are young people, Werner,' she said. 'There's no company for you here now Bartel Gurtnelli's gone.'

The Gurtnellis had not come back to the village. Bartel was now the youngest waiter at a big hotel in Glarmatt. Werner had looked in to see him yesterday before he went along to Glarmatt station.

'All the best,' said Bartel, 'and give them my best wishes.' Something in his voice made Werner think: 'He envies me.'

Bartel stood staring after him till Werner had turned the corner of the village street near the new bridge over the stream. A little farther on Bonzetti stood in the sunny street, gossiping with his neighbour the tobacconist. Werner read the name Bonzetti above the shop and saw the sun dancing on the pairs of spectacles in the window. He smiled and remembered Paolo and Aunt Augusta's spectacles. 'What a long time ago it seems,' he thought. 'They've built up their smashed houses much quicker here than we have at home.'

The train stopped at Brachen for three minutes. A waiter came out of the restaurant carrying a tray full of cups of coffee, followed by a waitress in a black dress with a white apron, with sandwiches and chocolates to sell to the passengers.

Werner shook his head. 'It hardly seems real any more.'

Then he began thinking of Marie again. He had seen her two days before, sitting knitting in Aunt Augusta's little room where the curtains were always drawn and it smelled of cats. She had been sitting in a dark corner and as soon as the bell rang in the shop she jumped up. As soon as the child was out of the room Aunt Augusta said:

'She's a dear little girl, but she isn't really happy with me. And I'm too old to change my ways. I see that now.' Two tears rolled down her thin, wrinkled cheeks and Werner was sorry for her. 'And I looked forward so much to having her,' she added.

Werner told her that he was going up to the children's village which was not far from where Klaus and Marie's grandparents lived, but she shook her head. 'It's no good, my dear boy. The grandparents haven't room for her as well. I wrote to them.'

Werner was so astonished he could hardly hide it. So Paolo had been right. 'All prickly outside and as soft as toasted cheese inside.' And her own nephew had never guessed.

'Auntie –' he began.

But she held up a shaky hand.

'I'm an old woman, Werner, and I've made a mistake. Your dark-haired little friend was right after all. You mustn't think I didn't think about it all a great deal, in hospital and after I came out, but I had the feeling that she was *my* child now – I felt *I* had a child now, like other women. I thought heaven had arranged things for me like that, but I must have read the signs wrong. She mustn't stay here, Werner. After all, she's an orphan. Perhaps they'll take her at that children's village where your friends live. Do your best for her when you get there, won't you, Werner?'

Two more tears rolled down. She felt for a handkerchief and Werner watched with the greatest interest, but it was not the one Paolo had given her.

Aunt Augusta smiled through her tears and said:

'No. That one's in my chest of drawers. It was a present. I haven't had very many presents in my life.'

★

And now here he was striding up the hill surrounded by the shrill chorus of children's voices with the deep notes of Antti's bass sounding now and then.

'There!' Tishoo pointed. 'That's where we live!'

Werner saw a group of large chalets with big windows standing on a broad slope above the brilliant meadows.

'There are lots more than you can see from here,' said Jean Pierre just behind him.

There was pride in the children's voices. This was *their* village. 'Look, you can see our football field over there, and that old shed is ours too. And over there on that slope we've built a ski-jump. You'll never guess which of us is the worst at jumping,' said Jean Pierre.

Paolo, who was walking in front in silence, for he had not yet got over his disappointment, threw a scornful look over his shoulder.

'Paolo!' Werner guessed at once.

The boys laughed.

'Paolo skis very well,' Tishoo defended him.

'He skis all right but he can't jump for toffee,' said Antti quietly. 'His skis flap like a donkey's ears. For jumping you've got to be a Finn, not an Italian.'

'What about Martin, then?' demanded the girl with the long fair plaits

'Oh, yes!' said Paolo over his shoulder. 'These people who can do everything perfectly are such a frightful bore. Martin can do this and Martin can do that and Martin can do the other, and when we dress up and play the fool at Carnival time he thinks he's the funniest of the lot, when really he is about as funny as a sick headache.'

'Now don't start quarrelling,' said Tishoo. 'I say, Werner, you didn't think this was the sort of place where people never quarrel, did you?'

Werner grinned. He found it all very amusing.

They had reached the village by now and were walking along the street between the houses.

'Look, this is where *I* live,' announced Paolo. He pointed. 'Do you see those sunflowers?' He slapped his chest. '*I* sowed those. The hollyhocks are Giuseppe's, and the small plants at the end were sown by three of the little ones in our house.'

'And that's our community centre, with a big room for parties,' said Jussi, pointing. 'Our Finnish house is just behind. And here's the office and the Head's house.'

'Where are we going now?' asked Tishoo.

'We're making a round trip first,' said Paolo, 'and then,' he added solemnly, 'Werner is invited to dinner at the Italian house. You're to come too, Tishoo, because we expected Marie as well.'

Werner drew Paolo a little to one side.

'I say, I do so want you to myself for a few minutes,' he whispered.

'We'll give them the slip presently,' Paolo whispered back. 'I've something to talk to you about too.'

★

That afternoon they lay side by side in the grass. They had walked right up into the upland meadows, which were much less steep than near Urteli. They lay down in the shadow of some spruce firs, where they could look down on to the children's village below them and to Trogen still farther down the valley. Lower still lay St Gall on the main railway line, with Lake Constance to the north.

'It's pretty here,' said Werner. 'It is at home, too, but our mountains are much more bleak.'

'We didn't come up here to talk about the landscape,' said Paolo. 'Spit it out. Why hasn't Marie come with you?'

'Because I wanted to talk to the people here about her first,' answered Werner with his eyes on a little cloud that was drifting across the blue sky. 'Doesn't the winter seem far away now it's summer time at last.'

'I'm not interested in the seasons,' said Paolo. 'What's up with Marie?'

'She isn't happy,' said Werner.

'Well?' asked Paolo in a strained voice. He was playing with a flowering grass. The stem was clenched between his teeth and by moving his cheeks he made the feathery plume swing to and fro in front of his eyes.

He's just as nervous as I am, thought Werner.

'Couldn't she come here?' he burst out.

Paolo squinted at the feathery plume.

'I told you that last winter,' he said more coolly than he felt.

'But what have we got to *do* about it?' asked Werner.

Paolo slowly took the piece of grass out of his mouth and looked at Werner in triumph. 'Klaus is probably coming here anyway,' he informed his friend in a voice of extreme satisfaction. 'Antti and I went to see him; we saved up our pocket money for weeks and weeks to pay our fare. I got his address from the Red Cross, because I forgot all about it when we all had to pack up and go off so quickly after that time we all went to see him in hospital at Brachen and he howled so. I got the address in a letter with a wonderful envelope addressed to Mr Paolo Fanfonnetti, and the others all laughed at me and said I was poking my nose into other people's business as usual. Antti was the only one who understood. So he came with me one Sunday. Mr Hutamäki knew about it and got leave for us to go.' He paused and bit fiercely at the grass stem. 'I think perhaps it was a good thing you didn't see him. He was quite ill with homesickness and didn't look much better than he did in hospital. His granny and grandfather were both of them old and ill. I've seen poor people in Italy; my granny's poor enough, heaven knows, but I'd never have believed that here in Switzerland there could be such ghastly slums as I saw there. Klaus recognized us at once and began to cry like a baby. Later Mr Hutamäki went there – it was frightfully decent of him. So he saw it all for himself and then he talked it over with the people who run our village. Then he went and saw them again, and the grandfather had to fill in forms and sign papers and things. And then an application for admission was sent in and Mr Hutamäki said what a pity it was only for him, the two of them ought to be together.' Paolo looked round at Werner and they both began to smile. Paolo flung away his piece of grass and said with a chuckle, 'If that stack of forms doesn't convince them, I don't know what will. Come with me and see the Head this afternoon. He's always ready to talk things over with us. He's a frightfully decent type.'

Werner rolled over on to his back again and now, strange to say, he had a grass stem in his mouth too. There was a pause before he said rather uncertainly:

'Do you think I could get a job here? I've done an

electrician's course in Zurich. D'you think there's a job here I can do?'

Paolo jumped up. He dragged Werner to his feet and said:

'Come on! Hurry up! At once! Hans Peter's gone and they've no one to take his place!' He started off, dragging Werner with him, but in his hurry he tripped over a tree stump and fell sprawling. Werner fell over him and they both rolled over in the grass, shaking with laughter. Werner had never felt so happy and carefree. Everything was part of it: the blue summer sky, the flowers, the buzzing of the bees, Paolo lying there in the grass kicking like a foal, and the prospect of living among friends, friends from all over the world.

*

At the beginning of the following September, Werner went to start his job at the children's village, not as successor to Hans Peter but as assistant to the electrician in the village.

Klaus and Marie arrived five days later. They were taken to live in the Swiss–Polish house and welcomed with the village song:

> *If all the children in the world*
> *Held hands with one another . . .*

Paolo stood there holding a great bunch of flowers which this time had not been picked in vain, and Tishoo put a wreath of flowers on Marie's head. Tishoo had made it herself out of all the late summer flowers she could find. Klaus and Marie stood hand in hand, looking anxious and a bit bewildered. Werner was quite sorry for them and everyone was grateful to Paolo for playing the fool as usual.

'Now nobody interrupt!' he ordered and began with a flourish: 'Ladies and gentlemen! It gives me great pleasure to show you round our village, where children from all over the world live peacefully together like brothers and sisters. If

THE PESTALOZZI VILLAGE

That group of boys, speaking half a dozen different languages, who went for a ski-ing holiday to the high mountain hut at the beginning of this book, all came from the Pestalozzi Children's Village at Trogen – and it's a real place, in Switzerland. It was started in 1946, just after the war in Europe ended, to make a home for a few of the many, many children who had been left homeless and friendless by the fighting. It is still there and there are always more children who need its help than there are places for – OR MONEY. Now, this very minute, there are boys and girls there from Austria, Finland, France, Germany, Greece, Italy, Switzerland, Hungary, and even England.

Homes are important and so are countries, so children of the same nationality live together there, with people from their own country to teach and look after them. In that way they don't forget their mother-tongue, or the ways and customs of their own people. If it can possibly be managed, children go back to their own country for the summer holidays, and so they keep in touch and make a few friends 'at home'. At the same time they are growing up with children of all those other nations whose language is different, and who all have their own national customs. In time they make allowances for the differences between them, and learn to recognize what is important in belonging to a country, and how little nationality counts when they are all playing or working together ... as, for instance, in this story when the children had to pull together to save their own lives, to save each other's lives.

When they grow old enough, the Pestalozzi children return to their own countries, taking back to each one what they have learned of friendship and tolerance and under-

standing. And those are first things if we are all to learn how to bring lasting peace into the world.

The name of the Children's Village was given to it in honour of a famous Swiss, Heinrich Pestalozzi. He lived about a century and a half ago, and had unusual ideas about education in the world. He wanted to see them put into practice at once, but he knew that an experimental school (such as the Children's Village) cannot transform the world overnight. He knew that it must be firmly established so that the new ideas can take root and have time and opportunity to grow.

When this book was first published, a Pestalozzi Village was just being started in England, at Sedlescombe, in Sussex. It and the one at Trogen are the only two of these International Children's Villages in the whole world; and ours too has thriven and grown.

Early in 1963, a group of children came to it from the terrible happenings far away in Tibet. These children are taught their own religion, and to read and write their own language, while also learning English and our ordinary school subjects, so that in time they may be able to take their places in the local secondary schools. Groups of children have since come from India, Jordan, Thailand, Nigeria and Viet-Nam.

For them, and for the other children at Sedlescombe, much money is needed, needed always and regularly, if they are to have clothes, and food, and warmth, and an education. So, before you forget about the adventures which are so exciting in AVALANCHE, won't you see if you can do anything to help? With a little money you could buy the little ladybird brooch which is the Pestalozzi badge. You might get other people to buy them too. Or you might save some money to send. And *whether you have money or not you can help by taking a little time to be quiet and think about all these children and what they ought to have, and then to say a little prayer to God to ask his help.*

The ladybird lapel pin costs nine new pence, plus postage, and the ladybird brooch twelve new pence, plus postage. The address to write to is:

> *The Pestalozzi Children's Village Trust,*
> *Sedlescombe,*
> *Battle,*
> *Sussex.*

Your parents and other grown-up friends can get all the information they wish about this Trust by writing to that address.

ELEANOR GRAHAM

Another Puffin by
A. Rutgers van der Loeff

CHILDREN ON THE OREGON TRAIL

This book is based on the true life story of thirteen-year-old John Sager, who, with his family, was part of a covered wagon band of settlers who set out for the Far West of America in the summer of 1844.

His parents died on the journey and the other pioneers decided to turn off and take the easier way to California, but John with his six younger brothers and sisters left the safety of the wagon train to keep faith with his father's dream of opening up the West for American settlers. Together the children made the almost unbelievable journey across two rivers, through hostile Indian territory, and over the Cascade Mountains.

This is the story of the appalling hardships which they endured – and of the outcome of their courage.

Some other Puffins you might enjoy

HURRICANE

Andrew Salkey

'Those big black clouds up there mean one thing, big trouble later on. There's going to be the most *terrific* hurricane of all time, in about ten minutes in fact.'

How Joe and his family lived through the night of the hurricane and what happened afterwards make a thrilling story. It has all the flavour and atmosphere of Jamaica, where it is set, and the author is one of the foremost West Indian poets and writers.

WHAT ABOUT ME?

Gertie Evenhuis

Four years of war – blackouts, gunfire, threadbare clothes and harsh German voices blaring through the streets, voices that sounded frightening even when they sang – in that time Dirk had grown into a serious eleven-year-old who desperately wanted to have a share in the secret goings-on of his elder brother, to do something to push the German invaders out of their lovely Amsterdam.

But when he saw the deadly result of his actions he knew that the fear of the Germans he had felt before was just a shadow of the terror he was feeling now – for his brother, for himself and above all for the teacher whose life he had put in such peril.

POLLYANNA

Eleanor H. Porter

Miss Polly Harrington was forty now. She liked being alone and certainly didn't want her orphaned niece, Pollyanna, to live with her but she knew her duty.

Then Pollyanna arrived, with two fat braids of flaxen hair, an eager freckled face, and her own particular magic – the Special Game she used to play with her father, the game of finding something in everything to be glad about, however bad it was.

One by one, as Pollyanna met the lonely, the sad, or the ill people in the town, she started them playing the 'glad game' with her too, and even Aunt Polly's heart began to thaw, until the day when something so dreadful happened that Pollyanna herself couldn't feel glad any more.

SMITH

Leon Garfield

Smith, the pickpocket, was twelve years old and he lived in the mazy slums round St Paul's. One day an old gentleman came up Ludgate Hill. His pockets bulged provokingly, and in an instant Smith had emptied them – but at that moment two men in brown appeared. The taller came at the old man from the front, the other took on his back – and slid a knife into it.

A quarter of a mile off, Smith stopped running. What had he got this time? Something valuable. Something that had been worth the old gentleman's life. He fished it out. A document. He stood up, spat, and cursed. He could not read.

But Smith hung on to his document. Hounded through London, pursued by the brown murderers, befriended by a blind magistrate, betrayed and flung wretchedly into Newgate gaol, he still hoped there might be something in it for him. And in a way there was.

MY SIDE OF THE MOUNTAIN

Jean George

'I am on my mountain in a tree home that people have passed without knowing I am here. The house is a hemlock tree six feet in diameter. I came upon it last summer and dug and burnt it out until I made a snug home in the tree.

'My bed is on the right. On the left is a small fireplace with a chimney that leads the smoke out through a knothole. It snowed all day yesterday and today. It must be below zero outside, and yet I can sit here inside my tree and write with bare hands. It is the fourth of December, I think. It is eight months since I ran away from home.'

This is part of Sam Gribley's diary. Sam had run away from home to live on the barren farm his grandfather had owned in the Catskill Mountains. He had a pen-knife, an axe, a ball of string, and some flint and steel, and that was all.

THE BONNY PIT LADDIE

Frederick Grice

Dick had expected to follow his father and his brother into the mine. Mining seemed the only natural employment for boys in the pit village where he lived, where people could hear dull subterranean sounds from the mines below the floors of their houses, and boys explored ancient deserted shafts as one of their entertainments. And Dick had never even questioned this way of life until the night he helped back to his home the owner of the mine, when he was taken ill, and began to wonder by what right Mr Sleath lived so well and held such power over his workers' lives. But it took a bitter strike and a dangerous pit accident to make Dick break loose from the pit for his future.

WATCH ALL NIGHT

John Foster

Tess is an only child, quiet and introspective. After a bout of anaemia, she is allowed to go to London for a few days to see her father, a nuclear scientist who works in an Arab state governed by a military dictatorship. She is enjoying her trip, until a number of frightening things happen. Her father disappears, then the hotel staff claim that she checked in alone, and when Ingrid the chambermaid also disappears, Tess is left to unravel the mystery and prove that she is not going mad. A gripping novel, filmed by Granada Television.

Heard about the Puffin Club?

. . . it's a way of finding out more about Puffin books and authors, of winning prizes (in competitions), sharing jokes, a secret code, and perhaps seeing your name in print! When you join you get a copy of our magazine, *Puffin Post*, sent to you four times a year, a badge and a membership book.

For details of subscription and an application form, send a stamped addressed envelope to:

The Puffin Club Dept A
Penguin Books Limited
Bath Road
Harmondsworth
Middlesex UB7 ODA

and if you live in Australia, please write to:

The Australian Puffin Club
Penguin Books Australia Limited
P.O. Box 257
Ringwood
Victoria 3134